NANCY WARREN

KARMA CAMELLIA

VILLAGE FLOWER SHOP
COZY MYSTERY - BOOK 2

Ambleside Publishing

INTRODUCTION

Murder lurks behind the prettiest blooms...

The past doesn't always stay in the past. Deeds can come back to haunt us. That's what happens to florist Peony Bellefleur's protégé and young witch, Char, when her old boyfriend turns up out of the blue saying he wants another chance. Turns out he's really on the run from crime. Meanwhile there's a competition among some of the women in the Cotswold village of Willow Waters to support the church vicar, a widower who graciously accepts everything from home-baked bread to hand-embroidered vestments. Is someone too competitive?

Life in the charming village may look picture-perfect on the outside, but like the camellias now in bloom, there can be stinging insects hiding amongst the perfect petals.

If you haven't met Rafe Crosyer yet, he's the gorgeous, sexy vampire in *The Vampire Knitting Club* series. You can get his origin story free when you join Nancy's no-spam newsletter at NancyWarrenAuthor.com.

Come join Nancy in her private Facebook group where we talk about books, knitting, pets and life. www.facebook.com/groups/NancyWarrenKnitwits

KARMA CAMELLIA

CHAPTER 1

*W*e could learn a lot from flowers. Unlike us humans, they don't hold grudges. They bloom, offering their beauty and scent, then fade away until the following year when they bloom all over again. They give everything and take nothing. They're selfless that way. As I said, we could learn a lot from flowers.

As both a witch and the proprietor of Bewitching Blooms, I also know that flowers transcend beauty and scent. As delightful as they are to the senses, each individual blossom symbolizes a different emotion for us. Aster for patience, freesia for innocence and caring, lilac for youthful exuberance. It's been that way for centuries. And, since you already know I tend to add a little benevolent witchy magic to my bouquets, they can speed the healing of the ill, add more festivity to a wedding or birthday party, and offer comfort to the bereaved during a funeral.

We might say someone's as beautiful as a rose or as fresh as a daisy, but in reality, people and flowers don't actually have that much in common. Especially when it comes to holding on to old hurts. You could step on a flower, run your lawnmower over it, accidentally let your dog pee on it—all of which I've done, believe me—and the flower doesn't complain. It might wilt or perhaps die for that season, but, in most cases, given a bit of encouragement and the right kind of nourishment, it will come back and give as much beauty, scent, and pleasure as before. In some cases, it will offer even more. I suppose what I mean to say is that flowers are extraordinarily forgiving.

People, on the other hand, can be a lot meaner.

And they do hold grudges. Sometimes for decades.

I was ruminating on this while admiring a beautiful pink and white variegated camellia, which was growing triumphantly in my back garden. If you don't already know, the camellia is a symbol of love and adoration, and boy, did it bring out the adoration in me. My garden in the Cotswold farmhouse where I live was a constant joy as well as a challenge to me. As you will have figured out, I love flowers. I love to watch them grow and see them bloom—enough to open a florist shop. And yes, okay, I admit I talk to them as well. There's no harm in that—as long as no one overhears you. I think my chatter makes them bloom a little brighter, frankly. Who doesn't want a little encouragement?

It was a particularly happy Sunday afternoon in May. The sun was shimmering and my housemates—Hilary, a former lawyer who was now spending her retirement taking a degree in Classics, and my sort of protégé, Charity, who preferred being called Char, *thank you very much*—were lounging on the patio furniture and doubled up in laughter.

Why? Well, we have Norman to thank for this particular spate of giggles, Norman being Char's familiar—a talking parrot who didn't only talk. He had a smart mouth and a sarcastic streak. He was a blue-and-yellow macaw and possibly one of the most annoying familiars in all of witchcraft history. That bird was a born performer and the best mimic I'd ever heard. Right now, he was doing a fantastic job of imitating my mom, Jessie Rae. She was oblivious.

Jessie Rae, a Scottish medium from a long line of mediums, appeared to be having a conversation with thin air. It sounds strange, I know, but with my mom, this kind of thing was a commonplace occurrence. The perfect word to describe my mom is ethereal. She's as slight as a sprite, with long red hair, and she doesn't walk so much as waft. She communicates with spirits, and the expression 'off with the fairies' pretty much describes Jessie Rae. She wasn't actually talking to the air; she was communing with a spirit. No doubt she'd come back to earth soon and let us know what nuggets of knowledge she'd received from the other side. Sometimes the messages made sense, other times...less so. But her gift made my mom unique, and we're all about that in my home.

My own familiar, Blue—a cozy marmalade cat who loved napping in the sun—was doing just that, not far from where I was attempting a little weeding. My weeding was halfhearted as I far preferred having a chat with the newly blooming camellias, reminding them how much I appreciated them and how beautiful they were. You know, nothing weird.

As I murmured and pulled up a pesky clover leaf, I felt for a moment as though the temperature had dropped by a degree, as sometimes happens when a cloud obscures the sun temporarily. Then a shiver ran down the back of my neck, and I knew it wasn't weather-related. I stood up slowly, shaded my eyes with my hand, and scanned the drive that led from the old farmhouse to the main road.

Sure enough, a lone figure stopped and stared and then seemed to consult his phone. I sighed. It was likely to be a tourist, blindly following Google Maps, which had accidentally sent him here. It happened all the time. Too frequently for my liking, since I had a lot that I liked to keep undercover at home. I hoped that the stranger had simply misread the address and would keep going, but, unfortunately, he'd seen me now and made his way toward me.

I squinted through the sunshine. The man was definitely a stranger to me. Tall, broad-shouldered, and muscular, he wore a tight black T-shirt with cut-off sleeves, which exposed his muscular arms, and blue jeans with a slash across the left knee. Everything about him said young, tough, don't mess with me. But I also sensed fear and a vulnerability buried deep within him. In my experience, those two qualities tended not to be great combinations. A frightened man will act out in a way a secure and confident one wouldn't.

He was probably in his mid to late twenties, and what I'd initially thought was a beard turned out to be a tattoo that covered the whole of his neck. It looked like a snake wrapped in barbed wire. Not designed to be beautiful, that was for sure. He walked decidedly toward me, his stance slightly bow-legged, as though he'd left his horse tethered around the corner, though I suspected in his case it was a motorcycle.

Was I intimidated? No. I've learned that appearances can be deceiving. And don't worry—I had a spell ready to stop him in his tracks if it became necessary. But as I stood my ground, waiting, my skin prickled with unease. Finally, he paused about three feet away from me and did his own squinting back at me. Something about his stare made my whole body shiver.

He opened his mouth, but before he could say anything, Char let out a wild shriek. "Mick?"

He turned at the sound of her voice and so did I.

Char's expression was a strange combination of delighted and horrified. She cried out again, "Mick? What are you *doing* here?"

Was this the old boyfriend Char had told me about? The one caught up in a bad crowd? My nerves prickled. I was ready to act all tiger-mom if necessary.

He narrowed his eyes at her, not running forward to scoop her up in his arms as I sensed Char was half expecting him to. I felt he wasn't sure what he wanted to do.

Finally, he said, "Babe." His voice was higher than I'd expected, with a scratchy quality that lent it an air of uncertainty.

The woman who wouldn't allow herself to be called Charity seemed to have no problem with babe. She walked forward, but she didn't throw her arms around him, either.

He stood there another moment and then said, "I needed to see you."

Char swallowed and then tightened the elastic which held back her pink-tipped hair.

I'm not sure any of us consciously realized we were doing it, but Jessie Rae broke off her conversations with thin air and slowly made her way toward us. Hilary put down the clippers she'd been using to cut rosemary for tonight's dinner, and Norman left his perch in an apple tree and quickly swooped down to sit on Char's shoulder. I'd never seen that bird move so fast. Normally Char would push him away, but this time she didn't. Quietly, we all aligned ourselves behind the young witch.

With his strong jawline and hulking demeanor, I might have thought Mick brutish if it wasn't for his watchful, wary brown eyes. He stood his ground as if used to being subjected to judgment.

It was Norman who broke the silence. "Who's this wise guy?" he asked.

Norman tends to get a reaction from most people the first time they meet him. Today was no exception.

Mick coughed in surprise and then glared at the parrot. "Careful who you're calling a wise guy. You might not be plump enough to eat, but you'd roast nicely on the spit."

I bristled. I hadn't warmed to the man who'd barged his way onto my property without asking. Now I definitely didn't like him.

If his rudeness did anything, it created a bonding moment between Char and her familiar. She took a hand and covered Norman's claws where they were curved gently over her shoulder.

"He's with me. What are you doing here, Mick?"

I wondered how he knew Char was even here. Had they been in contact, or had he sought her out? Even Blue now roused herself and wandered over to circle around my legs. My magic was always more powerful when my familiar was with me, so I was happy to pick her up and hold her tight to my chest. Her green eyes blinked at Mick. He now stared at this line of women and familiars and shook his head. I guessed we made for a strange sight, but Mick needed to know who he was dealing with. Cross one of my motley crew, cross us all.

"Came to visit you, didn't I?"

But Char wasn't having it. "What for?"

He sniffed, ran a hand under his nose. "Missed you."

Char scoffed. "But you dumped me."

"Man can make a mistake, can't he?"

Char was silent. She appeared to be weighing his words, or else she was planning a takedown of epic proportions. I couldn't quite get a read on her, which instantly made me worried. And yet, one thing I felt for certain was that true love was not the reason that had brought this clearly troubled guy to my doorstep.

"Could we talk somewhere more private?" Mick glanced back at us.

But Char shook her head. "Anything you want to say to me, you can say in front of my friends."

Mick shifted from foot to foot. I couldn't figure out if he was embarrassed to try to win Char back in front of an audience or whether there was something else at play.

"I want another chance," he said quietly.

"Fat chance of that," Norman snapped.

Char's defiant expression morphed into something softer. Was she flattered? Tempted? Her eyes flooded with a warmth that surprised me. It might have been a long time since I'd felt the first flush of love, but I could still read the signs. Char had once had very strong feelings for this man. But he had hurt her.

I could see what attracted Char to Mick. He was a classic bad boy; she was a wannabe rebel. But was there a real bond between them?

But then Char shook her head. "Come off it, Mick. I know you better than that."

"Really, babe. Just give me another chance. I missed you."

"You still hanging with the old crowd?" Char asked.

"Come on, they're my mates."

"Then you should leave," she said.

If Mick was embarrassed, he didn't show it. His chin jutted out, and he flexed the muscles in his left arm almost unconsciously. He listened as Char reminded him that he'd gone to prison and when he got out, promised her he'd break with the old gang. "What happened to turning over a new leaf?" she asked, her hands imploring.

"That's why I'm here, isn't it?" he said.

As I listened, I realized I was proud of Char. In the short time she'd been in Willow Waters, she'd done some growing of her own. She wasn't falling back into her ex's beefy arms. She was listening to her instincts.

He studied the farmhouse and gardens and said, "You've obviously landed on your feet here. Surely there must be room for one more?"

At that, I cleared my throat. "You should be directing that question to me, not Char."

Mick apologized, introduced himself, and finally, he stuck out his hand.

I shook it. His skin was warm and the vulnerability I'd sensed earlier pulsed beneath the surface. He was clearly a bit of a bad seed, but I also believed in second chances. I didn't want to judge Mick on past mistakes alone.

I glanced back at Char, and this time, I could read her completely.

"You can't stay here, I'm afraid," I said, "but if you find somewhere else local, I might have some casual work around the place, which could bring in some cash."

Mick was obviously strong, and maybe it would do him some good to put in some honest labor around the farmhouse. And if he wasn't up to manual labor, then that would get him out of town and away from Char faster than anything else I could devise.

Mick agreed, and Char visibly relaxed. She wasn't the only one. Hilary and Jessie Rae breathed simultaneous sighs of relief.

"I'll be back, Char," Mick said, squeezing her arm.

"Don't hurry," Norman said.

But before Mick could leave, another male figure appeared by the side of the house.

"Owen," Char said, sounding warmer than she had when she saw her ex.

I had a feeling things were about to get complicated.

CHAPTER 2

"Owen," I called, waving hello.

It had been a couple of weeks since Owen Jones's criminal record led to him being suspected of murdering poor Alistair Fairfax, but even in that short amount of time, things had swung back to normal. He'd kept his job as a gardener at Lemmington House, the Fairfaxes' Grade II listed seventeenth-century manor, and he often dropped by my farmhouse to offer advice or a helping hand. Owen was a gifted gardener, and I respected his abilities. In turn, he took a vested interest in how my garden was progressing.

I also couldn't help but wonder if a certain Char had also caught his eye.

Owen was brandishing an enormous clump of blue delphiniums, which, in his Yorkshire accent, he explained was a cutting from a huge plant at Lemmington Manor. "They need to be divided every few years. Thought the blue would look pretty next to the peonies." Continually working out in the sun had tanned his skin deeply. It was only then he seemed to notice Mick. He set down the delphiniums.

"Thank you so much," I said. I always welcomed new blooms to my garden, especially if brought by someone who knew how to grow them best.

But Owen's attention was fixed on Mick. He frowned.

"This is an old friend of mine," Char explained.

Interesting that she felt the need to explain Mick's presence.

I watched the two men appraise each other. Owen was rugged, muscular, and very handsome. Mick was also rugged but with a jittery edge, where Owen was calm and confident. They both had tattoos and wore a similar outfit of jeans and T-shirt. And yet, everything about Owen was more natural, relaxed, whereas Mick was a self-styled bad boy. Maybe it was their age difference. Owen was a decade older and perhaps ten years ago he had been like Mick—in with the wrong crowd and in trouble with the law.

It had recently been revealed to the whole village that Owen had been hired right out of prison, but so far, the villagers had been surprisingly calm about the news. They knew Owen as the man he was rather than 'ex-con.'

The two men nodded at each other, and then I saw Owen stare at one of Mick's tattoos. Five simple dots on the inside of his wrist. It was identical to Owen's.

"Where did you do your time?" he asked.

"Penny thwart," Mick answered. "You?"

"Hounds, up north."

Hilary stepped forward. She'd worked as a magistrate after her career in law. "Out of curiosity, would either of you gentlemen mind explaining what the dots symbolize?"

I smiled. Hilary was inquisitive about everything and scared of nothing.

Mick shrugged. "The five dots represent that you're serving time. A friend on the inside did it for me, stick and poke style." He pointed to the four outer dots. "These represent the four walls of the prison. Then the middle dot is for us, the prisoner."

"So simple, but full of meaning," Hilary mused.

My mom, despite being partial to the company of younger men, had lost interest in the conversation and retreated to a sun lounger. Blue had followed suit and was curled up at her feet, which I took to mean that any danger had passed.

Maybe I'd been too tough denying Mick a room here at the farmhouse. I certainly had a few spare ones, but my instincts told me to act with caution where this young man was concerned. I didn't trust him—and that had nothing to do with his past. People made mistakes and, like I said, I believed in second chances. It was more to do with how he treated Char. Despite her defiant tone, I could tell Mick had hurt her. And anyone who hurt Char would have me to answer to now.

Without being asked what he'd done time for, Owen began to explain his own story of misspent youth. He told Mick that he'd run with a bad crowd when he was a lad and that got him into breaking and entering. Nothing violent, and no one was ever home at the time, but he regretted it every day. He spent three long years in prison.

"I didn't know it at the time," he said, "but it was the best thing that could have happened. It's where I learned to garden. When I was being released, the warden gave me a good reference, and that's how I got the job here. It's changed everything."

I smiled. Owen had leapt straight into big brother mode. He'd obviously spotted the more vulnerable side to Mick as well and wanted to pull him away from whatever path he was dangerously walking down.

Having told his tale, he was staring at Mick expectantly. I think we were all waiting to hear the younger man's story, except maybe Char, who presumably knew it already.

I thought he might make a smart answer and refuse to talk about his past, but after a few seconds, he said, "Got caught up in credit card fraud. I was just the lackey, really. A bit of muscle. But I got pulled down with the lot of them when they got busted. It was a stupid idea when you really think about it. They went round blocks of flats and took the envelopes with credit and debit cards in them from the bank. The boss was like, in his seventies, full head of white hair and the most immaculately dressed bloke you'll ever see—I mean, he bought expensive clothes from the big department stores in London—Harrods, Selfridges, you name it. He was so charming—the ladies loved him. He made thousands and thousands, racking up purchases on contactless and ordering stuff online to flog it again later. He was rolling in it, until bam—game over. Went down for ten years. Who knows if he'll make it out? Although, he's still pulling strings in there. Some habits never die. But he took us all down with him."

Maybe you're thinking what I was thinking—why would Mick give all this information away so readily? It was like he'd been waiting all day to tell his story. And to a bunch of strangers, no less. Was Mick lonely? Was that the vulnerability I was sensing? Or was he trying to garner sympathy? I'd encountered a few men in my lifetime who spun 'warts and all' stories hoping to form an instant trust, only to prove wildly untrustworthy when push came to shove.

Owen nodded thoughtfully. "Well, if you've learned your lesson, you'll get no trouble from me."

Mick visibly relaxed. His shoulders lost their tension, and he let his arms drop from where he'd folded them across his broad chest. "And now I want to start over, you know?" He paused. "Char's always told me I need to get away from my mates. I decided she's right. I'm hunting for a place to stay around here that's cheap."

I explained that I'd offered Mick some work around the farmhouse if he could find a place to stay.

Owen ran a hand through his thick mop of curls. He seemed to hesitate, then said, "I've got a two-bedroom cottage. You can stay with me. And I'll be keeping an eye on you. Making sure you keep yourself out of trouble." Owen's cottage was hidden away from Lemmington House, so the landowning gentry would never have to see the workers, and Owen would make certain the current owner, Gillian Fairfax, didn't catch sight of Mick staying with him.

Relief flooded Mick's face, and any semblance of toughness completely melted away. He had been worried, scared even, but now he had a safe place to sit out whatever trouble he was in. I couldn't decide if I was pleased for Mick or not. The clash of vulnerability and bravado playing out inside of Mick was a recipe for chaos.

And, above all else, I wanted to keep Char away from that kind of energy. She was only recently getting to grips with her powers as a witch, and she was in a raw, vulnerable space herself—even if she'd never admit it. Char needed time to understand her place in the world and learn how important it was. She had a great responsibility to use her powers properly and for good, and I didn't want her to become distracted by the past.

"You can start work straight away," Owen said, taking charge of this strange situation in a way which I very much welcomed. "Come help me plant these delphiniums." He turned to me. "Peony, where do you think they should go? I was thinking they'd look nice next to the peonies?"

I was touched that Owen was asking my opinion after the mess I made trying to grow my own peonies. I contemplated the mass of blue spikes of showy flowers, each with their long spur behind the petals. From experience, I knew that they were moderately difficult to grow, but worth all the effort because they were so beautiful. Of course, I agreed they should go wherever Owen suggested. As soon as I'd spoken, Owen ordered Mick to fetch a shovel which was leaning up against my garden shed. He pointed to where he should begin digging.

Mick looked shocked that he was being put to work so quickly. In contrast, Char's face was full of mirth. I imagined my own expression matched hers.

Sometimes a bit of hard work goes a long way. And working the earth with your hands was a great place to start. I always felt my most grounded and peaceful when I was caring for the garden—maybe even more than with the blooms in the flower shop, as business could get in the way. Nothing was as satisfying as planting a tiny seed and watching it grow into a plant or shrub or tree or flower.

I thought about how much we could all change given a new environment and the right nourishment. Change and growth were all down to the right ingredients—whether you had stalks and stems or arms and legs. I thought digging in the dirt was the perfect new job for Mick. What better way to escape a past of bad choices and a bad crowd? It had already done Owen Jones wonders.

My mom had once pointed out that Owen's aura was orange, which meant, among other things, that he was creative, independent, adventurous, resourceful, and a person who overcame challenges. It would be interesting to see what kind of read she got on Mick. Surely, I couldn't be the only one who sensed something shifty about Char's ex-boyfriend? I'd ask her as soon as Mick left the farmhouse. That Owen had taken him under his broad-shouldered wing was a relief.

Norman flew back to his perch on an apple tree, and Char came and stood next to me. "Thanks, Peony," she said quietly.

I sensed she wanted to say more, so I remained quiet. But Char just stared at me and smiled. Her one front tooth crossed the other ever so slightly, like it was taking a curtsey.

I told her she was welcome. That we sisters stick together.

Meanwhile, Owen was instructing Mick in the best way of turning over the soil without disturbing the other plants. Mick's expression of derision was deepening. But what could he do? He needed a hideaway. He'd been given one. He needed cash. Well, he had to work for that.

"Delphiniums like full sun to grow," Owen was explaining, "and they need moist but well-drained soil. Good drainage is a must, as any soggy conditions can cause root rot. We'll have to feed them with fertilizer for the first few weeks as they adjust to their new home."

Mick grunted. He was already sweating and squirming. I

guessed that those tight jeans didn't make things any easier for him.

"A little deeper," Owen continued, peering down at Mick's shoveling. "I'm going to fetch a trowel."

Owen came to where Char and I had been watching the men work. When he nodded at Char, a look passed between them.

Was Owen doing all of this for Char? When he'd come to stay the other week, I noticed—happily—how the two of them fell into easy conversation. They seemed to have a lot in common, and something about Owen's steady personality smoothed out Char's spiky edges. Or maybe Owen had the same misgivings about Mick as I did. I'd offered him some work as a favor to Char, but also because if he was around the farmhouse, then I could keep an eye on him, too. Perhaps the same was true for Owen—if he rented the other room in his cottage, then Owen would have a better chance of knowing what Mick was up to. And if he posed a challenge to Char's affections. I really hoped that he didn't.

Mick glanced over at us then and Char excused herself to go and speak to her ex. Owen watched her go.

As soon as she was out of earshot, Owen said, "What do you think of him? You've got good instincts about people. Me? I don't trust him."

"I'm trying to reserve judgment and believe he wants a fresh start," I replied. "But if I'm honest, I don't trust him either."

"I know his type. Too quick to tell you what you want to hear. Dodgy."

"Exactly."

"I'll show him how to garden, but I don't want him

working with me at Lemmington House with only Gillian Fairfax living there. I barely managed to keep that job. And besides..." He trailed off as he frowned at Mick.

His muscles were visibly rippling, and I realized that Owen thought Gillian might try to seduce Mick. I remembered, vividly, how she behaved with her handsome tennis instructor. Who was to say she'd be any different with an even younger man?

"Is there something more concrete he could do here?" Owen asked. "Something that'll take a while?"

I grinned. I had the perfect job in mind. "Not concrete, but rock-hard? I've been wanting to lay another stone path through the garden up to the herb patch."

"Perfect," he said. "He's got brawn, that one, and putting it to use laying old stone will do him some good, I'd say. I'll supervise Mick closely, and I've got a contact at the quarry. I can get the stone for you at a good price."

Since my finances were on the tight side, this was extremely good news.

I thanked Owen, and he went to tell Mick about our plan. I don't know about you, but I certainly wasn't sure where this odd partnership would lead. There was no doubt, however, that I felt a change was coming to Willow Waters. Whether it would be good or not, I couldn't yet tell.

CHAPTER 3

$\mathcal{I}$ know that, for most people, Monday mornings can be a hardship. There's the customary groan at the sound of the alarm, the bleary-eyed coffee-making, the shoveling of cereal or mindless crunching of toast before the commute to work begins. But—and I really don't mean to sound smug here—I truly loved Mondays. It was the day I got up super early and went to the wholesaler to buy stock for Bewitching Blooms. It was quite possibly one of my favorite things about running the store.

Now, let me tell you, not every florist shop is as meticulous (or controlling, as Imogen likes to tease me) as mine. Most independent stores will simply order their blooms online. A few photographs of the wares and a few clicks later and hey presto: a full store. But that's not how I liked to do things. Nope. I'm far too protective of my business for that.

The best parallel I can think of is that it's the same difference between going to the greengrocer and choosing your own ripe cantaloupe and having any old melon delivered to your door through online shopping. Of course, you might luck out and have the best, most juicy and fragrant cantaloupe selected for you. But mostly the packer will choose without thinking—ripe or green as they come, or even a crazy substitution when the cantaloupe is out of stock. Imagine how many orders they have to get through in one day. Cantaloupes or flowers, prime freshness counts. So that's why I preferred to be more hands-on. It was the same for my fruit and veggies as it was for the store.

I'm naturally an early riser, and there was nothing like walking through the huge nursery first thing on a Monday morning and choosing the crème de la crème for my customers. It was this kind of personal touch that I thought separated me from competitors.

I was lucky to live near a small wholesaler who allowed people to peruse and buy flowers from their grounds and greenhouses, as well as imports from across the globe. The guy I liked best was called Frankie, and striking deals with him was always fun. He loved a bit of banter and would playfully mimic my accent in the hopes that I'd cave and pay a higher price.

Obviously, he never won.

Instead, I'd haggle him down and then organize the delivery to Bewitching Blooms with them to take advantage of their refrigerated van—not to mention the brawn of the deliverymen. A full bucket of flowers can weigh twenty-plus kilos and sharing the load is welcome. Sometimes Imogen, my assistant and a brilliant florist, came with me, but mostly she preferred to get her full eight hours of sleep. I didn't mind. Choosing stock felt like a privilege rather than punishment, and I used the time to think more about how to expand my business as well as my own expertise.

This particular Monday, I was overcome with admiration for the Dutch peony tulips with their feathery, almost crimped edges in an array of delicate colors: pink, pale orange, cream. I bought fifty stems of the locally-grown *Alstroemeria* in hues of purple and bright orange, then fifty more of the creamy-white American Beauty chrysanthemum and white freesia and roses, and a larger pick of the beautiful pink Sarah Bernhardt peonies. I also purchased the mixed fragrant stocks, *Celosia Reprise Rose* (also known as cockscomb) in salmon pink and velvety red, which to me, have a gorgeous brain-like pattern.

Then I moved on to the bright yellow *Eremurus* (also known as desert candles) with their long spike-shaped flowers with strong stems. The numerous, tiny flowers run all the way up the top half of the stems and flower from the bottom upward. They were showy and unusual and often used in large wedding pedestals, and the wedding season was fast approaching.

Thinking of weddings, I added *Eryngium* (also known as sea holly). I knew from my mom that these ornamental cobalt-blue thistles were popular as Scottish wedding flowers, and in the neighboring villages, there was a large community of Scots who'd moved from the north. Then I couldn't resist including one of my favorites—*Carthamus* (also known as safflower), which is a thistle-like flower in orange and yellow.

And let's not forget about the greenery. Springy Cwebe asparagus fern, wide areca palms, and the wider fan-like chamaerops palms. Plenty of the slightly pointed leaves of the Aspidistra Milky Way named for its galactic green and white marbled surface, and a hundred stems of the creamy-green

Francee hosta leaves. I added all this to our usual orders for The Tudor Rose Inn.

Did I go overboard? Maybe. But my instinct was telling me that it was going to be a busy week ahead. And, in all my time on this earth, I had learned never to ignore my instinct. It was my greatest asset. Along with my winning smile.

I'm used to being thrifty—I've told you before that running a florist shop is not a get-rich-quick career, and since I'd been widowed so young, my finances were all on me. So I made sure to keep my spending inside my allotted budget. Something that Imogen complimented me on when I arrived at Bewitching Blooms, where she had already set up for the morning.

"I don't know how you do it," Imogen said with a shrug, picking a leaf from the fabric of her sleeve. Under the jade-colored shop apron, she was wearing a pistachio-green cardigan with tiny pearl buttons and a pair of high-waisted cream slacks. How she stayed so pristine throughout the day always impressed me. She oohed and aahed over my buys.

"I think it was all the hours and hours spent budgeting for the farmhouse," I replied. "Haggling over prices with carpenters and builders and electricians." I'd had to take over when I discovered my husband refused to bargain. "Jeremy was terrible—he'd accept the first price. So British! I had to step in and be more forthright, otherwise we would have bankrupted ourselves." I laughed at the memory. It was nice when ordinary things about Jeremy came back to me. His little foibles and irritations. It made me feel close to him even though he was gone.

Imogen gave me a strained smile. I could tell it made her

uncomfortable when I brought up Jeremy, but it was important to me to keep his memory alive.

I was about to attend to the weekly orders when Char burst through the door, Norman flapping behind her. She looked enraged, her usually pale cheeks flushed. This morning, she'd pulled her pink-tipped hair into two tight buns that sat on either side of her ears, from the lobes of which dangled silver paperclips. Dressed in her usual uniform of black T-shirt and tight jeans, she looked like a punk rock Princess Leia.

"What's happened?" I asked. My first thought was that something had already gone wrong with Mick. Had he turned up in the night or threatened her in some way? My heart began to race wildly. But to my relief, Char pointed at Norman.

"It's that insane bird." She spun to where Norman had settled on the edge of my countertop, using his beak to casually straighten a wing feather, like a macaw at peace with himself and the world.

I didn't believe the innocent act for a second.

"He's been pooping on the coffee shop's patio," Char continued. "Roberto's been getting complaints. He's furious, and you know what he's like when he goes off on someone. You can't get a word in."

"Normie," I chided, "that's very inconsiderate."

Norman flapped his pretty wings. "I get bored. It's target practice."

"You're gonna get me fired!" Char exploded. "Don't you see? It's going to ruin everything. I need this job."

I was surprised at how vehemently Char was upset. Could it be that Char was happier with her new life in sleepy

Willow Waters than she liked to let on? For once, she hadn't added *for my new life in London* to the end of her sentence.

I checked to see that Imogen wasn't in earshot, but luckily she was wrapping orders in the back. "Norman, you know this isn't part of being a familiar—you're a team and that means supporting Char, not putting her work in jeopardy. In fact, you should even make her powers stronger."

"How? When I'm not allowed inside where she works?" he drawled in a sulky New York accent. "I'm stuck outside in a tree. You try it. Boring."

I actually felt for the colorful familiar, but I also felt for Char. I gave him a stern look, and he agreed to stay out of sight for a while. "Why don't you explore the area?" I suggested. "See the sights. Just make sure you're still in swooping distance of Café Roberto in case Char needs you."

"Roger that," Norman said, and Char and I led him out of the shop.

"You're going to have to learn to get along," I said as we watched Norman's bright feathers spread into an impressive wingspan.

Char thanked me, promised she'd try to keep her temper, and returned to work a little happier. A job well done, I thought.

Outside, I noticed that the hanging baskets needed water and grabbed one of my favorite watering cans (yes, a girl *can* have a favorite watering can) and set about refreshing the soil. It had been Imogen's idea to hang baskets by the entrance of the store to tempt shoppers as well as bees. I liked to keep them bursting with color and full of glossy ivy leaves, which trailed down to the sidewalk. Imogen had been right—

passersby always commented on how pretty they looked and sometimes came inside to see what else we had to offer.

But for some reason, one basket always struggled, and I was busy whispering a sweet spell of encouragement when the vicar appeared from around the corner. Reverend William Wadlow was a pleasant-faced man in his fifties with dark-blue eyes and cropped salt-and-pepper hair. Extremely popular in the village, he had a flock of local women who did everything from bake him scones to embroider vestments for him to wear. It was another village custom (or oddity) I'd come to enjoy. It was heartwarming to see how they venerated his leadership.

"Good morning, Peony," he said in his jovial voice. "Working your usual magic, I see?"

I blinked twice. My magic? Did he know I was a witch? Could he—?

"On the hanging baskets," he said, quickly responding to my bewilderment. "You always make them look so pretty. Not quite sure how you do it. Mine never seem to bloom the way yours do. Must be why you own the flower store." He smiled to let me know he was teasing.

I let out my breath. "Ah well, tricks of the trade, Vicar. I'd be happy to take a look at your baskets if you'd like. Sometimes all they need is a bit of encouragement."

"How kind," he said. "Isn't the weather glorious this morning? I've not seen such a lovely May morning as today."

We gazed up at the sky, and I realized the vicar was right. Not a single cloud marred the blue. See—I told you Mondays could be good!

We stayed that way for a moment, soaking up the tranquility of a spring morning in Willow Waters, until the sound of rushing footsteps clattered across the cobbled high street.

"Oh, William!" a female voice called. "I'm so pleased to see you."

We turned at the same time to find Dolores Prescott hurrying out of her cottage, across from my shop, with a biscuit tin in her hands. Her mouth had a swipe of pearlescent pink lipstick and her gray hair was staticky from being recently combed. I had to stifle a laugh. Did Dolores have a crush on the vicar? She looked as if she'd made herself up for a date.

He greeted her with a friendly handshake, and her cheeks flushed the same shade as her lipstick as their hands met.

Dolores stepped back and tapped the biscuit tin. "I made these this morning. Since I know you're partial to a fresh biscuit with your tea, when I saw you crossing the street, I thought to myself, well, wouldn't William be tickled by a batch of fresh shortbread?"

"My favorite, as you well know, Dolores. Thank you so much. You make me feel very looked after."

He took the tin from her hands as another lady speed-walked toward us. I recognized her as Elizabeth Sanderson, president of the local chapter of the Women's Institute. Despite the early hour, she also looked as if she'd spent more than a few moments in front of the mirror before leaving home. Elizabeth was a heavyset woman with a sweet, kindly face and hair so blonde she must visit the salon every other week. She was hugging something wrapped in a blue gingham tight to the buttons of her coral-colored twinset, which matched her lips perfectly.

I glanced from Dolores to Elizabeth, a smile on my face.

Seemed that the vicar clearly had two admirers. Rivals, even. Who would win the battle for the vicar's affection? William Wadlow didn't appear to have a favorite. In fact, I got the feeling he accepted their offerings as their vicar rather than as a man. He'd been a widower for some time, as I understood, and I didn't sense he was interacting with either woman with any notion of ending his single state.

"Elizabeth," William said, greeting her with a warm smile and what I took to be a twinkle of mischief in his eye. "How does this fine morning meet you?"

"Very well, indeed." She flashed a set of pearly teeth that may, or may not, have been her own, and unwrapped the tea towel to reveal a gorgeous-looking loaf of bread, obviously homemade. "Fresh bread. A brown loaf, seeded, just how you like it." She thrust out the loaf like an offering.

William chuckled. "Goodness me, I'm spoiled today. How very kind of you, Elizabeth."

Elizabeth was staring hard at the biscuit tin in his hands. Then her gaze raised to meet Dolores's faint scowl. "I do so hope those aren't biscuits," Elizabeth said, her voice taking on a schoolmistress' tone. "Too much sugar isn't good for you, William. Our dear Hyacinth was always worrying."

I knew that Hyacinth was his late wife, but she'd died before I moved to Willow Waters. They'd been married for more than twenty years when he was suddenly left alone. Although Elizabeth and Dolores were a little intense, it was also sweet how they baked for him.

"A treat now and then does no harm," Dolores said defensively. "A man needs to be taken care of."

Elizabeth wrinkled her powdered nose and then turned

back to the vicar. "Wonderful sermon yesterday. A true comfort."

"Ah yes, Isaiah 40—Comfort My People. One of my personal favorites. I return to it often."

"*All people are like grass, but the word of God endures,*" Dolores recited.

Clearly, her sherry drinking hadn't affected her memory.

"Indeed," Elizabeth said solemnly before changing her tone entirely. "William, I've nearly finished embroidering the new altar cloth. It may have taken me a year, but every hour has been more than worth it. I think it's turned out to be quite special."

The vicar clapped his hands. "Wonderful. I cannot wait to see it. I know it's going to be spectacular."

"Speaking of which," Dolores said, "I shan't have long to go with your stole. The gold thread is beautiful on the green."

The vicar blinked as if bemused by all the attention but thanked both women graciously for their wares and their promised embroideries before politely excusing himself to continue with errands. I wished him a good afternoon and watched the two women as they gazed after his departing form. It was sweet to witness their adoration. But the moment soured when Dolores muttered that too much bread isn't good for a man, and Elizabeth snapped back about sugar again.

I tried to smooth over the moment. "You're both so thoughtful. The vicar is lucky to have such kind friends. As are you."

At this reminder, Dolores and Elizabeth smiled.

Dolores turned to Elizabeth. "Do you fancy a sherry in

my garden this afternoon? The magnolia is blooming, so it's especially lovely."

"Very tempting, my dear, but I must finish the last stitches on the altar cloth. I'm going to visit the church later to double-check the dimensions are perfect before I hem the piece. I want the cloth to be ready for the evening service on Wednesday."

Dolores looked downhearted but nodded, and Elizabeth said goodbye to us both.

I picked up my watering can, but as I was getting back to work, Dolores tapped me on the shoulder.

"One of your geraniums is wilting, dear." She pointed at the basket.

Hmm, that's exactly why I was giving it a nice, long drink of water. "Thank you, Dolores," I said politely.

I expected her to leave, but for some reason she was still hanging around. "Was there something I could help you with?"

"It's Elizabeth that needs the help. I know what you're thinking and you're right. It's pathetic the way Elizabeth chases after William like a love-sick puppy. And if she thinks that blonde hair dye is fooling anyone about her advanced age, she's vastly mistaken. Well, I could tell her, but I'm too good a friend. Wouldn't want to hurt her feelings."

And with that, Dolores went back to her cottage and left me with my mouth hanging open. Wow. Where had all that come from? Wasn't Dolores a little old herself to be as jealous as a schoolgirl?

CHAPTER 4

*A*s I walked through the shop door, Imogen raised her head from the serving desk. "Watch out for that one."

"Dolores?"

"Exactly. She has a history. And it isn't pretty."

"She seems lonely."

Imogen snipped a white rose and slid it into a beautiful all white bouquet she was working on. "I wouldn't feel too sorry for her. She's got a mean streak and for all her biscuit baking, she's caused a lot of trouble. Let me tell you about Dolores and the new churchwarden." Imogen could put together a bouquet and still tell a good story and, as we weren't too busy, I tidied up while listening.

"Dolores used to be the churchwarden. Way before your time. She was good at it, too. She was well-organized, always had the correct hymn numbers up, and made sure everything ran smoothly, but she wasn't liked. Not hard to imagine why." Imogen peered up from her bouquet and I nodded, but she still supplied several reasons why. "She has a sharp tongue and is a terrible gossip and a back-stabber."

Okay, I'd never warmed to the woman, and Norman didn't have a good word to say about her, but in fairness, Norman wasn't the easiest company either.

"When Dolores retired," Imogen continued, "everyone breathed a sigh of relief, and Bernard Drake took over. He was recently retired and a friend of my parents. A former music teacher. He gave me piano lessons when I was a kid. I was a terrible pianist, but he was a truly excellent warden—for the churchgoers and music students. Calm, well-organized. Everyone liked him."

"Wait, isn't the current churchwarden a woman?" I searched my mind for her name, but it had flown out of my head. I knew the warden because I liaised with her directly when Bewitching Blooms was commissioned for funerals or weddings at the church. "Rebecca...something?"

"Rebecca Miller. That's right. Bernard Drake only lasted a year. Couldn't stand Dolores interfering all the time. She made him so crazy that he gave up the role, even though he loved it. He had to have therapy and everything. Although it's not all bad because now he's the church organist. But you watch out for Dolores Prescott. She cuts people to ribbons." Imogen snipped the air with her clippers.

Although I knew she was joking, I shivered.

THE REST of the morning passed without incident. I visited Roberto's café for our usual coffees. And I surprised myself by feeling disappointed that Alex Stanford wasn't there. Since our joint foray into investigating Alistair Fairfax's death, Alex often crossed my thoughts. He was tall, dark, handsome—and titled. The total package.

But there was something mysterious about him, too. It was more than the reclusive reputation he had in the village. More than my continued failure to understand how his title worked, Baron of Fitzlupin, from the ancient barony of Fitzlupin, how his surname was Stanford, but his title was Lord Fitzlupin. The whole British title thing was a complete mystery to me, no matter how many times Imogen tried to explain it all.

But no one, including me, could explain how I felt about his piercing gray-blue eyes. I returned with coffees for Imogen and me, wondering if he'd gotten under my skin.

I guess he must have because at that moment, the door opened and in walked Lord Fitzlupin aka Alex Stanford.

Okay, okay, I know what you're thinking. Too much of a coincidence, right? But listen, I'm nothing if not my mother's daughter. It was likely that Alex had popped into my head because he was on his way here already.

"Hello, Peony," he said, pushing a pair of dark Ray-Ban sunglasses up into his thick head of dark hair. The sun was shining through the windows and the light caught a few silver streaks in the black. They dazzled. He stopped and sniffed. "You went to the wholesaler this morning. Seems early for dahlias."

As always, I was floored by his incredible sense of smell. Dahlias are so delicately perfumed. "Hothouse grown," I said as a way of explaining his powers.

"Ah." He glanced around, and I wondered if he was planning to order flowers. Then he said, "Sorry to interrupt your work day, but I was hoping to ask you a favor."

"Of course," I said. "Let me set these in water." I gestured to the anemone which I'd been arranging into a wildflower bouquet.

"So, how can I help?" I asked, passing Alex a stool and sitting down myself.

"You know I'm in the wine business?"

"Yes." That was about all I knew about what he did in his spare time.

"I import wines from all over the world. I've been wooing an intriguing new client, or possible client. A French wine-maker who has refused to import his wine into the UK before, as he believes the English have no appreciation for the finer things."

I burst out laughing at that last bit, but Alex clearly didn't share my mirth. His face was deadpan. I felt chagrined and quickly apologized. "It just sounds a little..."

"Snooty?" This time Alex smiled. "I know. But his wines are so out of this world that I can almost forgive it. Which is lucky because somehow I've managed to impress him."

"That'll be down to your famous sense of smell."

Alex touched the tip of his nose and nodded.

"It still amazes me that you can spot a particular flower's aroma quicker than I can."

Alex tipped his head in modesty, but that man really did have an uncanny sniffer.

"I can identify the flowers, but I can't arrange them. That's why I'm here. The winemaker, Louis Gagneux, insists on coming to my home."

Alex did not sound happy about this. Our local lord was a

famous recluse. No one had seen inside his castle. He kept well clear of village affairs. He was a Willow Waters mystery. This must be his worst nightmare.

"Gagneux wants to view my wine cellars and my home. He's, shall we say, a little quirky, and that's how he makes up his mind who he works with."

"Well, that's one way of making a decision." I raised my eyebrows. Was this Gagneux just trying to get a glimpse behind the famously closed stone walls? Alex's castle fell just short of having a drawbridge, but if it did, the thing would be permanently pulled up.

"Which leads me to you, Peony."

I held my breath in anticipation and trepidation.

"I've visited him at his chateau in Burgundy, and there's no comparison. His grounds have Versailles, and mine have a dried-up moat. Could you come and take a gander? I was thinking that if we filled the place with flowers, it might look much better. In fact, the whole place could use sprucing up."

I inhaled deeply. "Flowers are magical but you know..."

"Yes." He shifted his stance as if uncomfortable. "I sense that my home needs...a woman's touch."

Holy Hellebore! Was Lord Fitzlupin blushing?

Well, I wasn't going to make things any more difficult for the man. "I'd be honored, Alex. How does tomorrow work for you?"

He sighed with relief and thanked me. I felt like saying the pleasure was all mine. Such an honor had never been bestowed on anyone in Willow Waters. Hilary and Jessie Rae were going to squeal—like I wanted to squeal.

But I didn't have a chance. Alex had barely left when Gillian Fairfax strolled in. I was surprised to see her as she'd been keeping herself to herself since being recently widowed. Besides, she wasn't exactly the most popular woman in the village. Gillian now lived all alone at the enormous, and much admired, Lemmington House, with only her gardener, Owen Jones, and a maid for company.

"Gillian," I said, cool and professional. "How can I help you?"

Gillian gently checked the sleek blonde chignon nestled at the nape of her neck. She was a very attractive woman in her forties who wore her wealth. Today Gillian was clad in an exceedingly chic white silk shirt with pearl buttons and navy slacks. She sighed in what sounded like real pain. "I've joined the Women's Institute, and it's my turn to do the flowers for the church on Sunday."

Gillian Fairfax did not seem like the WI type. My shock must have shown because she lowered her voice and said, "Frankly, I'm doing penance."

Immediately, I softened toward Gillian. In recent weeks, she'd been humbled by death and scandal, and her previous snobbishness had melted. At least partly. Why, she seemed almost human.

"Can you make me something lovely?" she asked in a soft voice. "I honestly don't care what's in it, or don't know what to ask for. But I'll pay whatever you ask."

To be perfectly honest, this was a dream commission for Bewitching Blooms, but it wasn't the only reason I wanted to be of help. It was pretty clear to me that Gillian was trying to get the notoriously cliquey women of the WI to like her so she could rub shoulders with the villagers a tad more amiably now that her husband was gone.

And that was something I could relate to. After I was

widowed, I stood out like a sore American thumb in this quiet and cliquey English Cotswold village.

Gillian shrugged. "The gossips had a field day, of course, when my affair was revealed. If I'm going to stay in Willow Waters, I'll have to find a way to fit in. The WI seemed the best bet."

I told her I understood and promised to make her the best arrangement I could. Plus, I had insider knowledge. "Something traditional and bountiful, but not too flashy, is your best bet. The WI women are very fond of white freesia. You'd do well to include a few of those." I began to circle our display, showing her the blooms that could pass as having been freshly picked from untamed gardens. I suggested tulips, lisianthus, veronica, daisies, and dragon snaps in pinks and whites with a splash of purple.

It only took me a few moments to talk through my ideas for an impressive but natural-looking arrangement, but Gillian's attention had drifted to something on her phone.

I cleared my throat, and she glanced up from her screen apologetically.

"I'll make up the bouquet on Saturday," I said, "so it'll be fresh for Sunday. You can pick them up anytime in the afternoon." I also suggested tying the bouquet with a pink satin bow.

She nodded and thanked me. But then she seemed to hesitate. "Do you think it's enough? Do we need more?"

I told her the bouquet was already reaching the one hundred and fifty mark, but she told me to increase it to two hundred and passed me her credit card. She really did want to impress these women.

Gillian was paying when Dolores walked in. I had to stifle

a sigh. My gaze went to where Norman had so far been perched peacefully and mercifully quietly on a ceiling beam. I could have sworn I saw that bird squeeze his wings close to his body and make himself even smaller. Not even Dolores's former pet wanted to chat with her.

Gillian turned and wished Dolores a good afternoon. But Dolores did not take it upon herself to return the pleasantry. Instead, she narrowed her eyes as she saw me hand Gillian back her card. "Are you ordering flowers for the church?" she asked.

"Yes," Gillian replied.

"When it's my turn," Dolores simpered, "I always make my bouquet from the flowers I grow specially."

Gillian stiffened. But Dolores held her gaze. It was icy and sent shivers down my spine.

"I'll come back later, Peony," Dolores said, "when you're not so busy." And with that, she disappeared out the door.

Two sightings of Dolores in one day? I must have some bad karma.

"She's the worst of the gossips," Gillian muttered as soon as she was sure Dolores was out of earshot. "Why, that woman would run me out of town with tar and feathers if she could. I doubt I'll ever fit in so long as she's around."

I assured Gillian that most people who lived in Willow Waters were fair-minded. And I determined that when I made up Gillian's enormous bouquet, I'd put an extra dose of magical goodwill into the blooms.

As soon as Gillian left, Dolores came back into the store. She must have been hovering outside.

"What can I help you with?" I asked politely, willing it to be a quick task.

"Does *that woman*," Dolores spat, "think she can buy herself popularity? After the scandal she caused? I don't know how she can show her face."

"Doesn't everyone deserve a second chance?" I asked.

She sniffed. "Gillian Fairfax doesn't even do her own flowers. People round here have respect for the homemade. Spending time and energy on arranging their own bouquets, not whacking everything on the plastic."

"How can I help you, Dolores?" I repeated, trying to sound cordial—and inspire the sentiment in return.

Clearly, I'd failed because a smirk appeared on Dolores's mean mouth. "I thought you should know, I saw several schoolboys stealing your flowers. Nasty little hooligans."

"Oh, Dolores," I said, in the sweetest tone I could muster, "do you mean from the bucket outside? That's where I leave the slightly overblown flowers that still have life in them rather than throwing them away. There's a FREE sign on the bucket."

Dolores looked stunned.

"I particularly like to see the children taking them—they often give the flowers to their mothers or teachers. It's very sweet, really."

"A better lesson would be for them to save up their pocket money. They have to learn that nothing is truly free in this life."

I counted silently to ten.

Dolores left without a further word and within moments, I saw her rooting around in the free bucket and crossing the road with more than her fair share of flowers.

"Char can be a pain in the backside," Norman muttered,

as he flew down from his perch to sit on my shoulder. "But she's got nothing on *that* woman."

"Quite right, my friend. Quite right." I sighed. "And speaking of pains in the backside, I should go and check on Mick's progress in my garden."

CHAPTER 5

*W*hen I got home, Blue greeted me at the door, mewing and rubbing herself at my ankles. I bent down and picked her up. "Just came to check on the boys," I said into her fur.

I wanted to see if Mick and Owen had made any progress on the stone path. I'll be straight with you: I wasn't entirely comfortable with Mick hanging around the farmhouse, even under Owen's watchful eye. Something about Char's ex was off and I hadn't been able to shake the feeling all morning.

I walked into the kitchen, the scent of the cinnamon and maple porridge Hilary liked so much in the morning still lingering, and out through the back doors into the garden.

There I found a somewhat sullen Mick slowly laying stones with Owen's supervision. Whatever the circumstances around me getting the path, I was thrilled to see it taking shape.

I called out hello and asked if they'd like some coffee. Owen thanked me and I went to put the kettle on. Blue stayed close to my side, which I knew meant that she was feeling my caution.

"You're a good girl," I cooed. "I know you'd far rather be snoozing than following me around."

Blue meowed in response. I figured she was saying, *Thanks. I expect a treat later.*

I took the coffee out to the men and asked if Gillian had minded Owen taking a Monday off to help here.

Owen scoffed. "Day off? Gillian's lucky that I still work for her at all. I care for the Lemmington House grounds seven days a week. It's pure loyalty to Mr. Fairfax."

I knew that Owen wasn't especially fond of Gillian after the recent widow fired him and then hired him back without too much of an apology.

I told him that she'd come into the store today. "She seemed to be quite different from her usual self. More humble."

"Is that so? Can't say I've noticed myself. But then I try my best to keep out of her way. She didn't exactly keep quiet about the fact that Mr. Fairfax hired me out of prison."

I frowned. Hadn't Gillian just complained to me about the perils of local gossips?

"Have you had any trouble? I mean, trouble round here means sarcastic asides, but still."

Owen shook his head and took a sip of coffee. "Honestly, I'm discovering that most people don't treat me any differently from the way they did before. I was so paranoid I'd be run out of town, but it seems like I didn't have anything to be afraid of."

I was happy that people could see he was a good man who'd made a mistake. I couldn't help but compare him with

Mick, who was huffing and puffing, and appeared anything but grateful for Owen's help. Was he a good man who'd made a mistake?

Mick sat down on a pretty bench to drink his coffee.

"You all right there?" I asked.

He grimaced into the sun. "I'm exhausted. The work is killing me."

"Mate," Owen replied, "we've barely even started. Put your back into it, and I'll buy you a pint this evening at the pub."

"Cheers." At least my unwilling laborer perked up at that.

Satisfied that all was well, I said goodbye, made a quick sandwich, which I ate standing by the sink, and headed back to Bewitching Blooms.

I tried to find compassion for Mick, but it was like that door was closed. Locked and bolted. There was something lurking behind all those tattoos that could not be concealed with just ink. I figured only time would tell what that something was.

BACK AT THE STORE, I kept my head down and plowed through the week's standing orders with Imogen. We had the radio on, the sun pouring through the window, and I was lost in the peaceful rhythm of working with flowers. Such uncomplicated bliss couldn't last long, of course, not with Norman still hanging around, anyway.

He broke our concentration with an extraordinary screech as he flew to the shop window. "Just another nip of sherry, just another nip of sherry." His imitation was spot on.

"What is Dolores doing now?" I mused, walking to where Norman was still flapping at the window.

I peered over the display of peonies and caught sight of Elizabeth Sanderson and Dolores heading for the church. Elizabeth was carrying a hessian bag very carefully, as though it were precious crystal she was afraid to drop. I assumed she'd finished her endless embroidery for the church and was delivering early.

"Just another nip of sherry," Norman echoed.

And then I noticed that Dolores did seem to be walking very carefully. Had she had a few too many sherries?

"Isn't it kind of early for...a nip?"

"It's five o'clock somewhere, Cookie," Norman replied.

"Actually, it's five o'clock *here*," Imogen said, and I was surprised to see she was correct. The day had flown by. "You okay if I knock off? I have a date tonight."

"Of course. Have fun. I'll want details tomorrow. You go ahead and I'll close up."

"Thanks." Imogen took off her apron and headed for the door. The bell tinkled behind her, then the door opened again almost immediately.

"Char!" Norman called out, delighted. "You missed me." He flew over and perched on her shoulder.

"In your dreams," she said, but she stroked his tail with one finger as she spoke. She was bonding with her familiar whether she wanted to or not. Her next words were for me, however. "I want to check on Mick. Make sure he's doing a proper job. You and Owen are only helping him for my sake. I want to make certain he doesn't let you down."

I appreciated that she'd been worried about Mick, as I had been. "Why don't you head home now in my Range

Rover. The walk will do me good." I tossed her my car keys and locked the door behind her and Norman.

Now, I've already told you that witches are great empaths, but what they're not great at is cleaning. Well, okay, maybe it's just this witch. As well as my powers, it was a condition that my mother Jessie Rae had passed down to me.

Growing up, Jessie Rae had never kept a tidy home. Sure, she burned incense so that the place always smelled of herbs and patchouli, and it was warmly lit with many colored paper lanterns, but sweeping, mopping, and dusting—well, I never saw any of that. It must have happened, of course. We didn't live in filth, but I've always suspected that my mom roped one of her friends into casting a potent cleaning spell on our place once the dust had gathered along the edges of the gold-framed oil paintings.

I'd had to learn how to keep things clean and organized at college, much to the chagrin of my roommate. Her name was Essie, and she'd patiently shown me the best way to fold my clothes and polish the limited furniture we had. But I'd never really taken to it. I preferred to make things pretty.

If you're wondering why I don't cast a teensy spell of my own, well, let's just say that my scruples are more firmly fixed than Jessie Rae's. I chose to abide by the coven rules and not cast spells for personal gain. It was a karma thing. And an honor thing.

Sweeping the last of the leaves into the dustpan and shoving the lot in the compost, I considered the day's hard work done. I tallied the cash till and the card reader, shut down the computer, and locked the store behind me.

The air outside was still wonderfully mild for six o'clock, and I was glad that Char had taken my car. Despite the gentle pace of life in Willow Waters, it felt like I was always dashing from one thing to the next. Orders, deliveries, a village meeting, buying groceries, picking Jessie Rae up from a séance evening, gathering herbs from Amanda to make tonics. Always something! Sadly, it meant I was often driving when I loved walking.

I'd grown up with a love of the outdoors. Maybe you've visited it yourself, but let me tell you, Maine has world-class hiking trails—and it's not just because that's my birthplace. Craggy coastlines, gorgeous foliage, and a variety of summits. I used to hike with my friends in Acadia National Park, where we'd trek up (and down) the mammoth Cadillac Mountain. Its peak is burnished gold by the first rays of daylight to touch the United States, and it's the perfect place to catch the sunrise year-round. No wonder I ended up in such a hilly part of England.

It was going to take me about forty minutes to reach the farmhouse. At this time of day, the high street was winding down its bustling business and handing the reins over to the pubs and restaurants for the evening. Although we were small, Willow Waters was home to some great restaurants which were fully booked throughout the high season, even with the inflated prices. My favorite place to dine was *Luce e Limoni,* a delight of Sicilian cuisine, whose homemade pasta I could happily eat every night. Specifically, the bucatini with spiced Sicilian pork-belly ragu. I had dreams about that tender meat. In fact, I was drooling just thinking about it and decided to make a little ragu of my own tonight for Char and Hilary. Maybe Owen would join us, and yes, Mick, too.

There was pork in the freezer—all I'd need was some good quality tomatoes. I turned left and headed for the greengrocer. Even though I knew it was past closing time, I had an intuition that it would still be open. Don't ask me why —my powers can extend to the possibility of tomatoes as well as more serious subject matters.

Up ahead, the owner, Liza, was bringing in the baskets of fresh produce from outside her store. I waved, and she shifted a bundle of asparagus to her left hip and waved back.

"Finishing late, too?" she asked as I sped toward her.

I nodded. "It's been busy for a Monday."

"Me too, though I'm not complaining. I sold through my entire week's order of chanterelles. Posh people and their posh mushrooms." Liza was in her mid-forties and her shoulder-length dark hair had beautiful streaks of gray running through it. The greengrocer had been in the family for generations. She ran the business with her husband, Don, who came from a family of farmers.

I told her about my sudden craving for ragu.

And she said she had the perfect heirloom tomatoes. "They're sweet but rich, too, and will cook down a treat."

She disappeared inside, and I paused to sniff the head of a cantaloupe for ripeness. If only I had Alex's sense of smell, then I'd always choose the sweetest one. I picked one, hoping for the best, and took it inside to purchase along with the tomatoes. A nice slice of fresh fruit after a heavy pasta meal would be perfect.

I thanked Liza and headed toward home with my purchases. Up ahead, the setting sun cast warm orange rays onto the old church. There was a slight breeze, and the leafy trees which flanked the building danced gently. And then the sound of singing carried across the air. Sometimes this village felt like it had a magic all of its own. Sweet, high voices trembled and swelled, and I caught the words of *'Be thou my vision.'* I realized it must be choir practice this evening. That's where Dolores and Elizabeth were headed earlier.

I paused for a moment near the entrance of the church and listened. I wasn't musical myself, so I appreciated the talent in others all the more. And the sound of the choir, all those different people working together to create such harmony, really blew me away. But this ragu wasn't going to make itself, and I still had some way to go.

I turned from the church to take the path which would lead me home when suddenly a piercing scream shattered the choral music.

The voices straggled and then stopped singing. But the screaming continued. I dropped the bag of tomatoes and the cantaloupe and ran toward the door, hoping someone knew more first aid than I did.

CHAPTER 6

*T*ime seemed to slow down as I rushed through the dim entrance of the church. The screaming persisted, shrill and haunting. I didn't know what I was thinking as I dashed in there. It was like my feet took over and the rest of me followed. Someone was in trouble or pain, and I wanted to help. I needed to help.

It was hard to see what was happening. Something had shifted inside the atmosphere of the church. Usually, the history of the church overwhelmed my senses when I stepped in. Built in the 1300s, it had been through many renovations over the years, and I felt its vibrations across time. But now the vibrations were quiet. All that I could sense was a deep anguish and the echo of a shrill scream which had not stopped.

Countless scenarios ran through my mind, but still—I was surprised to see that the scream was coming from the always-composed Elizabeth Sanderson. In fact, she was standing by the altar in near hysterics. Half of the choir members had gathered around her, but no one was doing anything. No one was even comforting her—they were stunned. What on earth was going on?

Another door at the side of the church opened and in rushed Reverend William Wadlow. We reached the altar at the same time and halted beside the wailing Elizabeth. The vicar's dark-blue eyes were full of concern.

"Elizabeth?" I asked. "Whatever's happened?"

The organist, Bernard Drake, and the rest of the women from choir practice now moved toward Elizabeth, who was openly crying now. She clutched her hands, wringing them tightly over and over. No words came from her mouth. Just sobs.

I still hadn't a clue what was going on. Surely nothing so terrible could happen at a wholesome choir rehearsal. I glanced from face to face. Everyone was pale. And still speechless. A few people avoided my gaze and stared at their feet.

And then I spotted Dolores. Her face was red, her eyes wide and alarmed. If she'd appeared to be tipsy when I'd seen her and Elizabeth walking earlier, then now she was stone-cold sober. And somber. She began to babble. "It was an accident. I was trying to get some light. Yes, some light. So you could see better. It was an accident."

But Elizabeth screamed back at her. "No! You evil woman. You ruined my altar cloth on purpose."

I followed Elizabeth's gaze and saw that an ornate goblet of communion wine had been knocked over onto the beautiful white altar cloth she'd spent a year stitching.

"Oh my," I whispered.

Poor Elizabeth. The cloth looked like it had been mortally wounded—the wine the same hue as blood. There was something especially terrible about something new being ruined in this historic place. Everywhere around us were artifacts, monuments to the past. Hanging above us was a Tudor altar cloth made from a number of fourteenth-century vestments stitched together, fishbone style. Overlooking the altar was a beautifully painted nativity scene. Beside that was a carved fourteenth-century stone seat bearing the arms of neighboring Cotswold villages. Even the organ was surrounded by medieval tiles salvaged from the nearby abbey.

Elizabeth had seen all this history and added to it. She'd given something made from love and devotion, an offering from the twenty-first century, to show that although times change, some things stay the same.

Dolores was shaking her head in denial while the terrible silence continued to fill the church, broken only by the sound of Elizabeth wailing. I made eye contact again with the vicar, who looked flabbergasted. I guess they don't prepare you for an embroidery disaster when you're training as a curate. Surely he had some wise words to share? Some comfort?

Then Rebecca Miller, the churchwarden, stepped into view. "Salt and cold water," she said. "Might stop the stain from setting. It's worked for me before. We must try."

"Right you are, Rebecca," the vicar said. "Right you are."

Everyone sprang into action, evidently to find some salt. Did a church keep salt knocking about? I had no idea. But clearly people wanted to help. Even Dolores, who seemed genuinely mortified by what had happened. She scuttled around, quite uselessly in fact—more like a chicken without its head than a friend on a mission. But I could tell she was trying.

Elizabeth, however, was inconsolable as we bustled

around her. She sank to her knees by the altar. "It's no use," she said. "It's ruined."

"Found a pack of salt in the office," the organist, Bernard Drake, called out.

"Pass it here," Rebecca said. "Let's see if I can work some magic."

Magic. Of course. I had a little experience of my own with red wine mischief and had had to help restore a few rugs and couches.

I stood closer, determined to imbue the cloth with healing properties without having to speak a spell.

"It was an accident," Dolores said again, screeching now. "I swear it. An accident. I would never."

Argh, that woman was breaking my concentration.

"Could happen to anyone," she continued. "I was only trying to help."

I closed my eyes and tried my best to close my ears as well. I needed silence to communicate this kind of spell. I felt the familiar warm buzz and let the words cross my mind's eye.

> *"To heal this cloth is what I seek*
> *Release Elizabeth from her plight*
> *I cast this spell to turn what's red to white*
> *To erase the damage and reverse the fright."*

There, even if I couldn't speak the words aloud, the concentration and intention should help the stain.

I opened my eyes to see Bernard Drake's very puzzled expression. My heart sank. I'd tried my best to not mouth the words, but had he caught me whispering to myself?

But no. Bernard wasn't looking at me. He was staring at the fallen goblet of wine. He scratched his head and then cleared his throat. "The communion wine is always locked in the vestry. How did it get into the chalice?" He glanced around and his gaze landed on Rebecca, who was bent over the cloth, still scrubbing with salt and cold water. "Rebecca, do you know?"

She glanced up and shrugged. As she was opening her mouth to say something, the vicar stepped forward and quietly suggested that it might be best for Dolores to go home.

Dolores stiffened like she might protest her innocence again, but instead, she began to cry.

It was a terrible sound. Now two women were crying— old friends at that. One in despair, the other full of sorrow. Were Dolores's tears crocodile tears? A way to garner sympathy following a false accusation? Or were they genuine tears of regret?

The entire church fell silent as we watched Dolores finally leave. It was a pitiful scene. Was she really so competitive she'd do something so mean within the confines of the church? It seemed odd to me, but then jealously was ugly and made people do ugly things. Dolores had a razor-sharp tongue at the best of times. Who knew how far she would go when pushed?

I peered over Rebecca's shoulder. "Is it budging?" I asked.

"A bit," she said, rubbing the salt and water mix into the dark strain. "Might take some time."

Some time and some magic: the best healing properties.

The vicar was trying to soothe Elizabeth, who—between

wails of despair—was still insisting Dolores had ruined her altar cloth deliberately.

"Dolores has left," he said in a soft voice. "I'll speak with her later, and we'll get to the bottom of this. But for now, come with me." He offered his hand and Elizabeth took it. He helped her to her feet and passed her an embroidered handkerchief.

"Oh, one of mine," she murmured. "How nice."

The vicar smiled. "I'll walk you home."

The two of them left arm in arm. It was a touching scene. The vicar clearly knew how to stay calm in any situation and offer comfort to those who needed it most.

I figured there was nothing else I could do and slipped away quietly to retrieve my poor abandoned bag of tomatoes and cantaloupe.

Outside, Elizabeth and the vicar were stepping onto the road. I hunted around for my goods. Luckily, the paper bag of tomatoes had stayed put. I checked inside: only one was squished. The cantaloupe proved to be more tricksy. Since the church was on a slight slope (like most of this village), I followed the downward incline until I saw the melon beneath an oak tree. I grabbed it and began making my way back to the farmhouse.

When I noticed the vicar and Elizabeth up ahead, I slowed my gait. I was surprised to see that the vicar still had his arm around her shoulders, but then I realized those shoulders were heaving. Elizabeth was still crying. She really wasn't taking this very well.

Following the same path, I could just make out their conversation.

"A year's work invested in that altar cloth," Elizabeth was

saying, "with my eyes failing and my poor hands stiff with arthritis. She's jealous of me. Always has been. Well, she won't get away with this. I'll see to that."

The vicar hushed Elizabeth and assured her that whatever Dolores had, or hadn't done, was for God to judge, not them. "Remember, Elizabeth," he said, "the Bible says, *But if you do not forgive others their sins, your Father will not forgive your sins*. Matthew 6:15."

"Yes, William, but I wonder if Matthew ever met a woman like Dolores."

CHAPTER 7

he next morning, I'd all but opened Bewitching Blooms' shutters when the phone rang. I'd arrived late as a foggy head was slowing me down. I'll admit to you, but perhaps not my customers, that I drank a little too much red wine last night while cooking the ragu. After the kerfuffle at the church, I returned to the farmhouse even later than intended.

As I'd suspected, after Owen and Mick had finished in the garden, Char had invited them inside for a drink. Hilary had locked herself away in her bedroom with her books. The ragu was fabulous, but as it simmered and bubbled away, the shared bottle of red went down fast and then another was opened. Hilary emerged in time for the pasta, and the five of us sat down to eat.

Despite my misgivings about Mick and his apparent aversion to hard work, he was a very polite dinner guest and appeared genuinely grateful for the meal. Thank goodness for the dishwasher. Owen finally drove them both back to his cottage at eleven, and I was about to fall into bed when Char had knocked on my bedroom door.

Not once since Char had started living with me had she knocked on my door. Worried, I opened it with a flick of my hand, too sleepy to leave my comfy position in bed and turn the handle myself. She came into the room a little sheepishly and apologized for disturbing me, but she wanted to show me something.

I immediately perked up. The next stage of her powers were in motion—I could feel it.

"Peony, look at this," she said, and with a turn of her wrists, she switched off every light in my room in one swoop.

I laughed into the darkness. "Brava!"

"What does it mean, though?" Char asked, clearly not as happy as me. She must have turned her wrists again because the lights came back on. Her face always looked younger after she'd washed away her makeup, and now she had the air of an anxious child. "I thought my power was about bringing light. And heat. Why else did I start shooting flames from my fingertips the other week?"

"It's a cycle, remember? The world works in circles. If you give out light and heat, you can also take it away."

Char frowned as if puzzled. "But last time I discovered a power, it was the Flower Moon. You told me that it was a time for me to bloom, accept my power, and pull the weeds that were taking up space in my life. It's not a full moon now, so why is this happening? I feel out of control."

I smiled, touched that Char had not only been listening, but that she'd remembered my advice. I told her that far from being out of control, she was, in fact, growing. I reiterated what had been said to her at the last full-moon coven.

Witches follow nature's seasons, the cycles of the moon, and commit themselves to work with the earth's elements—earth, air, fire, water—as well as themselves to shape their own life. If she continued to open herself up, her powers would keep growing.

So, as I was saying, I opened the store late and as I stepped through the door, the phone began to ring.

Norman was with me and he shrieked, "The early bird catches the worm," as I scrabbled for the phone.

I muttered my irritation, then shot back, "Why don't you put a worm in it? Isn't that just the kind of treat you like?"

"Cookie, come on," Norman replied in his most charming voice. "You know I'm a strict vegetarian."

He flapped around the store and then headed outside through the door I'd left open.

And I finally answered the phone. It was Dolores. She sounded terrible.

"I've been trying to reach you all morning," she said, her voice thick with emotion.

I glanced to where Norman had now taken a perch on one of my hanging baskets. I hoped his antics weren't going to put off customers. I could imagine him spitting out all kinds of rude comments about my customers' hairdos or choice of clothing before they'd even walked through the door.

"I opened a trifle late today," I said, yawning. "Sorry for the inconvenience."

"I need to send flowers. Right away. They're for Elizabeth."

Dolores sounded on the verge of tears. In fact, I couldn't recall a time—other than yesterday at the church—when I'd seen or heard her so emotional. I was far more used to her snarky tone, and it shook me up to hear her sounding so vulnerable. Whether Dolores had actually instigated the wine-spilling incident or not, being accused and publicly shamed as she was in the church must be taking its toll. Dolores was an old woman, but I didn't wish her any pain.

"I understand," I said softly. "Do you know what kind of flowers she likes?"

"Of course," Dolores said quickly. "I've been friends with her for years. Elizabeth loves calla lilies. White ones. And they'd better be fresh."

Hmm, there I was feeling sorry for Dolores when her tone rapidly switched back to patronizing. Now I felt more certain that the wine spill was no accident.

I told her that we had plenty of white calla lilies and then quoted the price per stem.

Dolores was silent. I waited. Nothing.

Sighing, I said, "I also have a ready-made bouquet with two white calla lilies, several roses, and baby's breath. Would you like one of those? It would be much cheaper."

Dolores was living on a pension, after all. I couldn't begrudge a more modest budget.

I told her the price, and she said, "Fine. If you'll deliver it to Elizabeth. I've never seen her so angry. She won't even take my calls so I can explain. The flowers will have to speak for me."

I did feel sorry for Dolores. She was in a real state. Not that she didn't deserve to be if she'd deliberately ruined Elizabeth's work. However, maybe it was an accident, or she really was penitent. Either way, it would be nice to help these two old friends patch things up.

So, I said, "Yes. I'll take the bouquet to Elizabeth myself, free of charge. It's only down the road." I couldn't believe I was waiving delivery costs for Dolores, but there you have it —never let it be said that I'm not a generous soul.

To her credit, Dolores was grateful and asked if I could write a message on the card as well.

"Of course. Hold on just a moment." I rooted around for a pen. Imogen was forever tucking them behind her ear and then leaving them someplace obscure. I could never find one when I really needed it. I pulled open each of the desk drawers until a lone green ballpoint appeared. "Okay, I'm back. What would you like your card to say?"

There was a pause and Dolores was thinking so hard I could hear it down the phone line. "My dear Elizabeth. I am very sorry the wine was spilled on your beautiful embroidery. It was the new warden's fault. I would never have left wine in the cup when I was warden. Your friend of many years, Dolores."

I frowned as I wrote the words. If you had to look up the definition of a 'sorry/not sorry' note in the dictionary, you'd find Dolores's attempt at an apology.

"I see," I murmured. But it wasn't up to me to judge.

If Dolores was going to insist on continuing to protest her innocence, then that was her business. I wrote the note according to Dolores's instructions and promised that I'd deliver the bouquet as soon as Imogen arrived for her shift. Without even thanking me, Dolores said goodbye and hung up.

I stared at the receiver, wondering why I'd done a favor for this woman. She really wasn't very nice. I only hoped the gesture would help mend a friendship because the Elizabeth

I'd seen wailing and then ranting last night had not been in a forgiving mood.

I consulted the clock, counting down the minutes until Imogen would arrive. We staggered our shift times so that some mornings she opened and others I did. We'd been trialing an open late on Thursdays for shopping, and today was her turn to do the late.

So far, the evenings had been pretty quiet, but the odd flurry of customers would arrive minutes before seven. And I'm sad to say it was usually men desperate to make a last-minute purchase for a birthday or anniversary. Or, of course, the usual 'I'm so sorry' flowers. But hey, the guilt they felt about almost forgetting, or being too late, could lead to zealous buying, which was great for the store. Anything to keep business healthy.

When Imogen arrived at ten, refusing to tell me anything about her date apart from the word 'disappointing,' I filled her in on the scandal of the altar cloth and Dolores's subsequent flower order. Imogen listened eagerly and was suitably horrified. She knew everyone and most of the village gossip. She was a native Willower, after all.

"Dolores Prescott can be truly vicious about people behind their backs, but even I wouldn't have thought she'd do anything so spiteful," she said, eyes wide. "Elizabeth Sanderson is a sweetheart. A bit intense, yes, but well-meaning. And they've been friends forever. I almost wonder if it was an accident. Maybe the warden did forget to return the wine to the vestry." She raised one of her perfectly plucked eyebrows.

How I wished I had Imogen's talent for silent skepticism and disapproval at the same time.

"I can believe that Dolores did it," I said. "Even in the past week, I've heard her say many a spiteful thing without flinching. But don't you think it seems strange to do something like that so publicly? And in a church, of all places? The whole choir was there as witnesses. And everyone knew how hard Elizabeth had worked on that altar cloth. It was her pride and joy."

Imogen seemed to consider this for a second and then said, "I wonder if it was a mad bout of jealousy. Really, they'd both be happier if they put their crush on the vicar to one side. Not that they're the only women in the village who seem to think he can't manage without their cakes and biscuits and invitations to dinner. But jealousy's an awful thing."

For now, I had to deliver Elizabeth's flowers. And Dolores's not very apologetic note. She hadn't specified what kind of card, so I did what I could by selecting one that had the words *I'm sorry* on it. If the message didn't give the right sentiment, maybe the card would.

I told Imogen that I'd suggested one of our ready-made white flower bunches for Elizabeth.

"Here," Imogen said, after rooting around to find the freshest one. "This should cheer up poor Elizabeth. I know she has a blue vase that these would fit nicely."

"Is there anything you don't know about our neighbors?"

"Nope," Imogen said with a cheeky grin.

But Imogen was right. The blue and white contrast was cheerfully stimulating. After witnessing Elizabeth's inconsolable weeping yesterday, I hoped that these might brighten her morning. And maybe Rebecca Miller had managed to salvage the cloth with cold water and salt, after all. Along with the extra help from my spell. If so, then a tragedy could be turned into an unfortunate incident.

I told Imogen I'd be back soon and set off for Elizabeth's house. She lived close to my mom's store, and I thought I'd pop in to say a quick hello to Jessie Rae as well.

CHAPTER 8

$\mathcal{I}$t was midmorning, and the weather was warm.
And I soon regretted the long-sleeved sweater I'd
donned. I'd chosen it for its color: a vivid green, which I
thought brightened my sleepy complexion and complimented all the foliage in the store. (Yes, I did try to tone with
blooms, what of it?) It was oversized and comfortable, even
when tucked into my black denim pencil skirt, but now I was
longing for a short-sleeved T-shirt.

I climbed the winding path which led me to Elizabeth's
house, but when I saw the candle burning in the window of
my mom's store, I felt drawn to say hello to her first. You
might call me sentimental, but after my musing about the
importance of sisterhood, I'd wanted to give my mom a hug.

Even on sunny days, my mom burned aromatherapy
candles, and I could see the flame flicker through the
window. Jessie Rae liked to set a sensual tone for shopping,
and there was often one candle, or even two, lit at a time. As I
pushed through the door, the chimes rang out, and I inhaled
the heady scent of sandalwood and jasmine.

Inside looked totally different from the last time I'd visited. Jessie Rae rearranged the store constantly—according to what the spirits thought was best. And the spirits seemed to be pretty contrary.

Today, the crystals had switched places with oracle and tarot cards. The wind-chime section had been refreshed and was now sitting next to the aromatherapy candles and incense. I also noticed that she'd color-coded the bookcase. Instead of being organized by genre and interest (which made the most sense), spines of a similar hue were neatly resting against one another. I guess one spirit must have been feeling particularly creative.

No one was inside the store.

"Mom?" I called out.

"Just at the reading table, dearie," Jessie Rae replied from behind a red velvet curtain she'd set up to hide a gorgeous Georgian dressing table, which she'd polished and repurposed for astrology and tarot readings.

Usually, she locked the store door during a reading so as not to be interrupted. It wasn't like her to forget. Or no, wait, that's not true. It's totally like my mom to forget.

Through the gap in the curtain, I was amazed to see Elizabeth Sanderson sitting with Jessie Rae. As far as I knew, Elizabeth had never set foot in my mom's store before. The occult wasn't very WI. Elizabeth was wearing a cream twinset with the neck wrapped in pearls with a blue clasp. Her cheeks were a vivid pink—more like she was embarrassed than heavy-handed with the blush. What was going on?

"Sorry to interrupt," I said, still trying to recover from my surprise. "How strange, Elizabeth, I was just on my way to you to deliver these." I gestured to the bouquet in my arms.

Any embarrassment that Elizabeth might have felt getting caught in the occult shop melted away at the sight of my blooms. Was my goodwill spell already working?

"Flowers?" she asked. "For me?" Elizabeth glowed. "Whoever from? Oh wait, is it from William? The vicar really is too kind. He always knows what to say and do."

But before I could answer that these flowers were actually from Elizabeth's currently least favorite person, Jessie Rae said, "How nice, dearie. Perhaps some cheery flowers will dissuade Elizabeth from continuing along her current path."

I now saw that my mom appeared troubled.

The glow disappeared from Elizabeth's cheeks. "Isn't there any customer confidentiality in this place?"

"Dearie, the spirits hear everything. There's no need for confidentiality. It's merely a construct. Besides, secrets do more harm than good."

I could feel Elizabeth's turmoil and recalled how badly upset she'd been when her altar cloth was damaged. "I'm so terribly sorry about what happened yesterday. Was the warden able to remove the stain?"

Elizabeth shook her head. Today, her blonde hair was frizzed wildly, and I wondered if it was from a night tossing and turning on her pillow. "Of course not. All my work is ruined," she said darkly.

"I was just in the middle of explaining to Elizabeth here," Jessie Rae said, "that we don't engage with dark spells."

My heart raced. That did not sound good. "Dark spells?"

No wonder Jessie Rae looked troubled. First, do no harm, and all that. "Yes, I think my lovely neighbor might have been a bit confused about what we do here. I told her that we don't have anything like that —especially nothing to do with..." She paused and shook her head sadly so that her long silver earrings brushed her shoulders. "Revenge."

"Oh, Elizabeth," I said softly, "This isn't going to make you feel better."

Elizabeth's color deepened, and she looked mortified, but there was something hard about her expression, too. Something determined. "That woman ruined my year's work. My beautiful cloth. Perhaps it seems silly to you, but she knew how much it meant to me. I know your mother has power. I've seen it. I want that woman to suffer as I have, and I'm determined to find a way."

Jessie Rae laid her hands palm down on the table, and I saw that she'd set out numerous crystals. "I was thinking, luvvie, that perhaps you might like a calming crystal instead." She picked up an amethyst. "We call this *the intuitive eye*. It's perfect for your predicament because it holds a great relaxing energy. Keeping this on your person will help you release your negativity. Aye, it'll even send pleasant and peaceful pulsing energy vibes through your body. This way, you can find some clarity. Once we have understanding, we can let go of the dark and let in the light. And then you'll feel much, much better."

Jessie Rae smiled, obviously pleased with her perfectly positive speech. She was, as I'm sure you can imagine, an excellent saleswoman because she had what they call *the gift of the gab*. There was no one like my mom for suggesting items that someone had no intention of buying and then convincing them to walk out with three.

Elizabeth cleared her throat. Clearly, this was not what she'd come here for, but she hadn't reckoned on Jessie Rae's insistence. Still clutching Elizabeth's flowers, I pulled up a stool and settled in for the show.

Of course, my mom was not about to be dissuaded.

"Or how about celestite?" she said, all smiles. "See how soothing the blue color is? It has high vibrations which clear away chaos to leave you with a sense of serenity. Who wouldn't go in for a little serenity, right?"

"I'm not sure that—" Elizabeth began, but Jessie Rae cut her off.

"Celestite connects to your third eye, heart, and crown-energy centers and creates a sense of safety and calmness, allowing you to let go of your fears and give in to release. Release feels so good, you know. No one wants to walk about carrying a heavy heart."

"I'm not heavy-hearted," Elizabeth said, more than a little exasperated now. "I'm upset."

"Then that's settled," Jessie Rae said, rubbing her palms together. "You'll take a fluorite for balance and clarity. It replaces negativity with a rational and clear mindset. It's got your name on it, my dearie."

Elizabeth sighed and picked up the purple and greenish-blue stone. She shrugged and murmured, "Yes, I'll take it."

I swear to you that my mom makes ninety percent of her sales by sheer force of will and an ability to completely ignore the reticence of her customers.

"Great choice," Jessie Rae said, standing and revealing the full effect of her black and silver dress. "I'll wrap that up for you. And how about a pound of my delicious toffee?"

Elizabeth nodded, keen to get out of there.

"Have you ever seen such an aura?" Jessie Rae whispered

as she walked past me. "Red and black. Terrible energy. I'll have to cleanse the shop the minute she leaves."

I didn't see auras the way my mom did, but I could feel the negative energy pulsing around Elizabeth. While my mom wrapped the crystal and the candy, I was able to hand Elizabeth her bouquet. After watching that scene, I was now extremely worried about how Elizabeth would take the good-will gesture. The mixture of anger and sadness radiated off of her in waves. I hoped the flowers might help soothe her fury at Dolores.

We all had to live together in this small village, after all.

Elizabeth opened the note hurriedly, and I realized I hadn't yet told her that the flowers weren't from the vicar. She was about to get a shock.

As her eyes scanned the page, reading the message from Dolores, her entire face fell.

Her cheeks went a deep and furious shade and, to my dismay, she tore the sorry/not sorry card into tiny pieces and let them flutter to the ground. It looked like ragged confetti, but we were about as far away from a celebration as could be imagined.

My mom gazed at us from the counter, her expression troubled. Elizabeth was about as far from serene as could be, and now Jessie Rae was lost for words—and believe me, that's not a common occurrence. There were never bad vibes like this in her store, and she was clearly out of her depth. I hoped she had plenty of sage to burn once Elizabeth had left.

"And as for these," Elizabeth said, holding out the flowers as if they were a used diaper, "pretty as they are, these flowers are nothing but a lie." She dropped the bouquet to the floor and, to my horror, she stepped on them hard.

I gasped. My sweet blooms! How *could* she? "Elizabeth," I breathed. "There's really no need to take your anger out on innocent flowers." I bristled and drew myself up to full height. Mess with my flowers, mess with me.

But Elizabeth ignored me completely. The flowers hadn't soothed; they'd inflamed. "You can keep your crystals and sweets, Jessie Rae," Elizabeth said, rising to her full height as well. "If you won't give me what I want, I'll find a revenge spell on the internet."

"You mustn't!" Jessie Rae called out as Elizabeth prepared to leave. "Negative spells come back three times as potent on those who use them. You could hurt yourself."

"I'll be taking my chances," Elizabeth said with a haughty tone, and to my dismay, she stomped over the bouquet and out of the shop, trampling my beautiful blooms further into the ground. The shop door jingled, and then there was silence.

"Oh dearie me, oh dearie me," Jessie Rae said, springing into action and picking up the crumpled bouquet from the floor. "What behavior. I've never seen the likes of it from her before. Och, she's acting like a stroppy teenager."

"All over a piece of embroidery," I said, shaking my head.

My mom clucked her tongue. "Worldly matters. Nothing important."

Perhaps it wasn't just worldly matters. Was this feud between friends charged by their mutual attraction to the vicar? Was that why Dolores ruined the altar cloth? Because she couldn't bear to see Elizabeth be praised so highly by the vicar?

My mom closed her eyes and began to sway. I held my

breath, knowing that a message was coming from the other side.

"Jessie Rae hears something. The spirits. They're in turmoil. Everything churning, churning like the ocean. Waves crashing, falling. Something drops like a pin in the water but ripples...everything ripples." She opened her eyes again and blinked three times. "Och, something's amiss."

I tried to make sense of her vision. But surely the spirits couldn't care about a spoiled altar cloth, as sad as it was. They had bigger fish to fry. "Was that a premonition about vengeance? Maybe Elizabeth is really set on cursing Dolores and it's going to end badly?"

"I don't know, dearie. Only that the spirits are riled. The spirits always know."

I rolled my eyes. Her riddles riled me no end. "But what do they know, Mom?"

Jessie Rae flicked her flaming hair back, her expression unfussed. "They work in mysterious ways, luvvie, you know that."

"Well, I do wish they'd be more direct with their communication." I picked up the abandoned fluorite crystal and rolled it between my palms.

The stone was smooth, the color changing from purple to green to blue as it hit the light. If Elizabeth wasn't open to a calming crystal, then we'd have to find another way to stop her from using dark magic to curse her friend. "She doesn't know what she's getting into," I said, as Jessie Rae began collecting sage and salt.

She was clearly planning a thorough cleansing spell, and who could blame her?

I cleaned up the poor, broken flowers, hoping that Elizabeth's violent outburst would prevent her from doing anything worse.

A revenge spell wasn't anything to mess around with.

CHAPTER 9

*A*fter the disaster of my flower delivery, I returned to the store unsettled and sadly put the ruined flowers in the compost. I didn't even take out the few that weren't ruined to put in my free flower bucket. I didn't want some innocent child taking home a flower that carried such angry energy. Best to let the blooms return to the earth and regenerate.

My mom was right. Elizabeth didn't know what darkness she might invoke. The internet was no place to learn spells. Especially not ones for revenge. Maybe I would visit her this evening, after she'd had time to calm down, and talk her out of any mischief.

Meanwhile, I had some important, and exciting, commissions to think about. Obviously, I'm talking about Alex. It was time to invest my energy dreaming up some impressive bouquets to charm Alex's potential French client.

I was looking forward to visiting his castle. I'll admit I was feeling inquisitive. Okay, nosy. Surely you can't blame me for wanting to see inside the castle of a notoriously private man?

But it was more than that. His was the kind of challenge I loved receiving at the store.

My favorite part of running Bewitching Blooms was working with people and creating something bespoke that would fit their occasion. The stranger the request, the more I loved to fulfill it. A bouquet for a child's first wobbly tooth? Sure. Something for a cat's birthday? Why, of course. If each flower had its own meaning—serenity, or passion, or good-will, for example—it wasn't so hard to combine stems that spelled out a personal message, so to speak. So, it comes as no surprise that I was delighted to sketch ideas for Alex and his castle. Of course, I wouldn't be able to execute a complete vision until I'd seen the place. But I could research Versailles and the types of flowers found in its garden. If Alex thought his client's house resembled Versailles, then I could summon some royal touches of my own.

As I Googled away, I discovered that Versailles was built more than three hundred years ago by the rulers of France as a monument to their imperial dominion. The grand palace and expansive gardens combined took up more space than Paris itself. I'd never visited Versailles and added it to the very long mental list of places I wanted to see. Especially the gardens which I wanted to learn about.

After a few minutes on the internet, I was ready to book a tour of Versailles. The extensive gardens were full of fountains, ponds, paths, and landscaped hedges—brought together in a design that harnessed water, earth, trees, and, of course, flowers. Together, they created vistas that stretched to every horizon. Off these grand avenues, the garden broke into groves. Gated and walled by greenery or trellises, the gardens were sectioned into 'outdoor living rooms' and built for the court to use as party rooms for musical entertainment and dancing.

I thought of the single path Mick and Owen were laying in my farmhouse garden. Okay, I was no Sun King, but I was doing my best with my vastly smaller space. I even had a pond. A single pond, but still. It encouraged frogs and birds and was a pleasing water feature.

Obviously, there wasn't much I could do for Alex on the walled garden and statue front, but I could suggest sectioning his grounds. As for the plants, color was the name of the game at Versailles—color and abundance. The upkeep of the palace was insane! Every year, 50,000 flowers were planted to fill all those acres with bright, glorious color.

Among the varieties planted, the tuberoses, jasmine, and pink carnations stood out to me. Tuberose and jasmine were both white waxy flowers with sumptuous perfume and were usually found in hot, balmy climates. One waft of their powerful scent and a sense of luxury and pleasure can overcome even the most hardened of souls and transport them to their holiday destination of choice. And if Alex's French client was the snob that he had hinted at, the man would be sure to love these elegant blooms.

As for the centerpiece bouquets' pink carnations, well, they weren't my favorites, so I thought I'd slip in my name-sake peonies, which had been freshly delivered this week. Who wouldn't be cheered by giant puffs of those crowd pleasers? And some bright pink camellias would comple-ment the peonies perfectly. If Alex wanted a feminine touch to brighten his dark castle, then this combination would be a good start.

The only thing which worried me was Alex's sensitive

nose. To my amazement, Alex could sniff out each individual bloom in the fragrant front room of my store. Would he be able to handle a castle full of powerful scents? Were the rooms big enough to dissipate the scent to just a hint? I'd know more when I arrived.

Armed with my sketchbook, I set out for the castle in my Range Rover, more than a little excitement bubbling away in my belly.

Fitzlupin Castle had been in the Stanford family for generations, and it was an undisputed architectural master-piece in Willow Waters. And in a beautiful Cotswold village where busloads of tourists snapped photos and oohed and aahed all summer long, that was saying something. Set back from the country lanes by way of a no-through road, the estate comprised a house, tower, and extensive outbuildings, including stables. All surrounded by that now dry medieval moat and gates, hedges, and fences that helped ensure Lord Fitzlupin's privacy. I pulled into the driveway and wound down my car window to press the intercom button.

"Hello, madam. How may I help you today?" a gravely formal voice asked.

Madam? I glanced around for the camera that'd given away who was waiting to be let in. Instead of the traditional lion mounted on a gatepost, I saw a stone wolf with the glint of a lens in one eye, staring down at me.

"Peony Bellefleur," I answered, "here to see Alex Stanford."

"Lord Fitzlupin is expecting you, Ms. Bellefleur."

I swallowed. Yes, I'm a doofus for not using Alex's proper title, but it's hard for this American gal to wrap her head around all the British aristocracy.

There was no time to dwell on my etiquette faux pas as the unwaveringly formal voice only paused for a beat before saying, "You may park beside the outbuilding on the left side of the house," and the iron gates slowly opened to reveal a grand driveway leading to the castle grounds.

I drove slowly, taking in my surroundings. As far as I knew, no one in the village had come this close to Alex's ancestral home. Rumors abounded—ghosts and hauntings, towers that weren't far from crumbling. Mysterious servants who never mixed with the locals. But as I parked by the outbuilding, I was instantly struck by the sense of how *solid* the castle was, how absolutely part of its environment. Of course, it was still an intimidating structure. It was a castle, after all. But it emanated security, a sense of belonging. It was reassuring rather than imposing, and I was pleasantly surprised.

Sketchbook in arm and tote bag over my shoulder, I approached the ancient front door. I'm not exaggerating when I tell you that it was about as high and wide as my entire garage and no doubt the wood was a foot or more thick. I pressed the modern buzzer, and my gaze drifted up to see another security camera. I swallowed again. But then I gave myself a mental shakedown.

I was Peony Bellefleur, and I had been through much more harrowing experiences than visiting a posh house.

After a moment, the door opened as slowly as the heavy iron gates, revealing an elderly man. His stately appearance matched the voice on the intercom when he said, "Welcome, Ms. Bellefleur." He was dressed in an outfit I'd only seen while watching Downton Abbey. Despite the warm day, he was wearing a starched white shirt, white bow tie, and a tailored black jacket with matching trousers. His shoes shone as bright as any full moon I'd seen, and his posture was erect and dignified. He was the very epitome of decorum.

"Please do come in," he said, as he stepped back to let me enter. If he was surprised that Alex had invited someone to the castle, his face showed no sign. But despite being heavily wrinkled, his gray eyes were sharp as a magpie's.

I tried to appear relaxed but truth be told, the inside of the castle was even more enormous than I'd imagined. No doubt this was because the place was bare. And I mean missing *all* the usual home comforts. As my gaze flicked across the enormous hallway's multiple doors, I noted that the wooden floors were worn and scratched as though a pack of dogs had run riot through the house. There was no ottoman, no chest of drawers, no lamps—only an ancient chandelier in serious need of dusting. It emitted a weak light, which half illuminated the gray stone walls.

I could see why Alex was worried about having a sophisticated Frenchman here. This place didn't feel like a home at all.

There was a creak as one of the doors opened, and then Alex emerged. He was dressed in his classic attire of a crisp button-down shirt and indigo jeans. I don't mind sharing that they looked great on him. His dark hair was slightly damp as though he'd recently showered, and as he came closer, I smelled a hint of his herby scent. My nose isn't as sharp as Alex's, but it's not bad.

"Ah, Peony," he said, smiling at me, "I see you've met George, my house manager."

From behind me, George scoffed and before I could

answer said, "I was butler to your father, and a butler to you, and I'll be a butler until the day I die."

Alex laughed softly. "House manager is more modern, don't you think, Peony? Butler sounds so..."

"Traditional, sir?" George answered. "And for good reason."

Alex smiled gamely, and I could tell this was a well-played bit between the two men. "Thank you, George. I can show Peony around from here."

George's footsteps disappeared up the enormous staircase at the other end of the entrance hall. I truly felt like I'd traveled back in time. Surely not much had changed here since the Middle Ages.

Alex faced me with raised eyebrows as if to say, *See, I told you so; I'm at a loss.*

"Don't look so worried," I assured him, laughing nervously. "It'll take some work, but I'm sure we can transform your castle. How much time do we have?"

Alex thanked me again for coming at such short notice and confirmed we only had a few days. Honestly, there weren't enough flowers in Versailles to make this barren room look like a home.

I asked for permission to take photos for reference. When he agreed, I put my sketchbook in my tote bag, took out my phone, and started snapping pictures.

I stayed silent as he led me through an enormous drawing room, taking it all in and listening as he narrated its incredible history. Here Alex's ancestors threw grand balls, which sometimes lasted entire weekends. He regaled me with stories of lavish dinners: suckling pigs and roasted ducks and suet puddings—whatever that was. I saw several charming antique sideboards, but the chairs and couches were well-worn, and there were no rugs or curtains. The room was as far from its lavish party past as I was from Maine!

The kitchen, on the other hand, was another story. Sleek, modern, and full of fancy-looking equipment, it was absolutely the heart of the home. Beautiful marble countertops offset the gray flagstone floor. There was storage galore: built-in cupboards painted a rich deep gray to match the flooring and a paler gray tiled splashback. Mixer, blender, pestle and mortar, a huge knife block, and an industrial-sized coffee machine lined one wall.

I stared at the machine for a moment, and realized it was close to the model Roberto used at his café. It struck me then that Alex really didn't need to go to Café Roberto for coffee every morning. He had the means for a perfect cup of joe right here. He must make the walk into town for some human connection. This recluse was perhaps not as reclusive as he liked people to think.

"Now this is something," I commented, walking around the kitchen. I didn't want to say it, but even the lead-piped windows sparkled cleaner in here than elsewhere.

Alex laughed. "Phew," he said, mock-wiping sweat from his brow. "You've smiled at last."

Oh dear. I really was going to have to work on my poker face. "It's beautiful," I said, taking in the high-end gas stove with well-loved pots and pans hanging above it, the double oven, the enormous stainless steel fridge, and the farmhouse sink.

This wasn't a show kitchen. Someone in the castle made complex meals here. I didn't see a cook, but no doubt there was a Mrs. Patmore, like on Downton Abbey, hiding away somewhere. Through a huge backdoor, I saw a garden with a thriving herb patch. Alex opened the door so I could see it better and, almost unconsciously, nipped off a sprig of rosemary and passed it to me. The dark-green spiky leaves were warm from the sun and smelled spicy and astringent. Bees were busily moving between lavender, mint, and sage.

He snipped a sprig of each and held them under his nose. "While you work out flowers, I'll plan the food."

And then I fell in. There was no Mrs. Patmore. I turned to him, smiling broadly. "Is this where you spend all of your time when at home?"

Alex appeared a touch embarrassed, like I'd discovered a secret. "I do love to cook. Although it's not always fun cooking for one. Or two, when George agrees to sit down to dinner with me."

"I know that feeling. When my husband passed, I never had the heart to cook properly for myself. Having Hilary and Char around makes dinnertime a lot more enjoyable."

Alex smiled, somewhat sadly I thought, and I kicked myself for reminding him of my full house. Had I made him feel lonely? But then, his single state was definitely his choice. I'd seen the way women looked at him. I'm pretty sure they saw me looking at him the same way.

He led me into the separate dining room. It smelled of must and damp. My kitchen excitement dipped. Unfortunately, his love of cooking didn't extend to the dining room. He must eat in the kitchen, or in some as yet hidden room where he kept a TV. Here the antiques were covered in drop sheets. The walls were graced with paintings, but they were all dull and dusty oils. Who wanted to eat dinner beneath the gaze of gloomy-faced ancestors?

The more Alex showed me around the castle, the deeper my heart sank at the thought of trying to turn this place into a warm and hospitable environment. The library was vast and impressive—full floor to ceiling shelves made of walnut, and lined with leather-bound hardbacks and separate rows of paperbacks. Yet there was only an old leather armchair and a very bland-looking table light by which to sit and read.

We headed back to the kitchen. It was indeed the most delightful room so far, and we took a seat on the counter stools. "It really is dreamy in here."

"I do love to cook," he said, "which is why I'm going to make dinner myself. The personal touch. I took a summer course in Tuscany one year, and I'm planning a feast. But something different from Italian food..." He stopped talking, and I wasn't sure if he hadn't decided on the courses or wanted the meal to be a surprise.

I was intrigued. "Whatever you prepare, I feel certain it will be delicious. You definitely have the kitchen for it."

Alex thanked me and without trying to disguise his trepidation said, "We have three days until the vintner comes for dinner on Friday. Do you think that's enough time to do something about this place?"

"Three days," I repeated, trying to arrange my features into a semblance of calm. "I'll arrange the flowers and plenty of them, but you're going to need a team of cleaners and interior designers to remove the drop sheets, clear the dust, and brighten the rooms with rugs and curtains and whatnot."

Alex nodded.

I scrabbled in my tote bag for my sketchbook. "I've already spent time thinking about flowers. And now that I've seen your place, I know I'm on the right track." I showed him my ideas—each bloom and bouquet sketched and labeled with descriptions.

He nodded as I talked him through my Versailles references. We sat side by side, and after a while, I could feel his eyes on me more than my sketchbook.

"True perfection," he said softly, and I couldn't help but glow at the compliment. "I trust you completely, Peony. Whatever you think is best."

The scent of him tickled my nose pleasantly. When I turned my head, we held each other's gaze. My stomach flipped.

Glancing away, I said, "From what you've said of the French vintner, every detail could be important. You'll want your silver polished to a high shine and your dining table set properly with your best china. Charger plates, starter plates, that kind of thing."

"Oh," Alex said. "I was planning to serve everything on ordinary dinnerware, but there is the family china with a crest on it and numerous table linens packed away." When he stood, I did as well, and he led me back to the dining room and an antique buffet by the fireplace.

That would need cleaning as well. Too warm for a fire, but perhaps another flower arrangement could brighten the space. I made a hasty note in my sketchbook and snapped more photos.

My jaw dropped as he opened the buffet to reveal all sorts of gorgeous dinnerware.

"After what you've said, I'm now certain I can't do this all by myself." He took out his phone and tapped and swiped and sighed disappointedly, as if searching for messages that weren't there. "I'm trying to arrange a London firm that stages houses for sale. They bring in everything. Timing's the issue, though. The woman said she'd get back to me today."

"Great idea," I said, but I was more focused on exploring the treasure inside the buffet. By my eye, his family china was custom Wedgwood, and the porcelain was hand-painted with the elaborate crest he'd so casually mentioned.

"There's some amazing stuff here, Alex. Your family has an incredible history." Privately, I thought he should take better care of what was no doubt priceless and irreplaceable history.

"If only I'd inherited their taste for finery," he said. "I prefer simpler things."

I unearthed a massive and truly beautiful crystal vase from the back of the buffet. "I'll fill this with flowers," I told him. "Are there any more?"

"Dozens, I should think. I'll get George to gather them."

I considered my options. "If I could have six cleaned and ready for Friday, I'll make them look less formal. We can use them to add color to any spots that need brightening." I kept my voice cheerful, but there were a lot of spots in the rooms I'd seen that needed cheering up. Still, it was only dinner for a client, not a royal wedding. I rezipped the cases containing the china and opened a set of doors lower down. Inside, there were piles of silver sheathed in thick protective plastic. I stood back and admired the haul.

Alex did not. Instead, he frowned at a charming chair pushed to one side of the buffet.

"That looks like it belongs at the head of the table." I pulled the chair into the light. "Oh," I said, studying its legs, which were marked with gouges. "What happened here? Has it been...chewed?"

"Must be the rescue dog," Alex said. "He's very excitable."

I'd completely forgotten about Alex's puppy. "Ah, of course. Where is he? I love dogs."

"Out for a walk," Alex said quickly. When his phone dinged, he just as quickly turned his attention to the device. "Shame you missed him. But happy news, there's a reply from the London house-staging company. If I pay a premium, they'll have the job done by Friday."

I smiled. "See, you hardly needed me at all."

Alex returned my smile. "On the contrary, I couldn't have done it without you. And the pièce de résistance will be the flowers, of course."

Despite myself, I blushed. Don't judge me—Alex is gorgeous, especially when he smiles. At me.

CHAPTER 10

Once we'd finished discussing final touches, Alex asked if I was heading back into town and when I said yes, he asked if I'd mind giving him a lift.

"I've a few things to pick up at the deli, and I told Roberto I'd test another batch of coffee he's imported," Alex explained, "but with all my worry over Louis Gagneux, I'd clean forgotten my promise. Better not to take two cars if we can avoid it—for the environment, you see. I try to do my bit."

"Sure," I said, nodding. I was surprised at how glad I was to keep our meeting going.

We walked out to my Range Rover and drove directly to the high street to make it to the coffeehouse before closing time.

As I drove, Alex told me more about the vintner, Monsieur Gagneux. His vineyard had been in the family for three generations, and his grand estate spanned forty hectares in the Languedoc region. "He loves his food, his wine, and sparkling conversation. Loathes exercise so you can imagine he's fairly rotund."

At that description, I laughed and told Alex he had a real knack for summarizing characters.

"But Louis does all the work for me," Alex said, chuckling. "He's a big personality. I hope he agrees to work with me. His wines would be an excellent addition to my portfolio, and I always prefer to do business with people I like." He glanced my way, and I felt included in the category of people he liked, which was nice to know.

It was wonderful to see Alex so open and relaxed this way.

"Gagneux is also one of life's great talkers, but that is only second to his impressive consumption of his own product. And I understand why. He does make the most fabulous wines. He has a blend of Carignan, Grenache, Merlot, and Cinsault, which is out of this world. Blackberries and spices, and flexible and soft tannins in the mouth. You'll have to try some."

I turned onto the high street and slowed as I approached my parking spot in front of Bewitching Blooms. "I have to admit that none of those words made much sense to me."

"We can drink a bottle this weekend if you'd like. Hopefully, a celebratory bottle to toast my new client."

"That sounds lovely." A warm feeling flooded me at the thought of sharing some wine—whatever the vintage or grape or grower—with Alex.

I parked, and Alex suggested we get a coffee and continue discussing the plans for Friday. I could see my shop was running smoothly, so I agreed, and we walked toward Café Roberto, chattering about the intensity of the scent of tuberose. Alex insisted he could handle the luxurious-smelling flowers.

We were so caught up in conversation that I almost jumped out of my skin as we passed Dolores's cottage, and someone came running so fast they'd have slammed right into me if I hadn't leapt out of the way.

"What the—?" I stopped, recognizing Mick, who should have been at my place working, not practicing sprinting drills on the high street.

"Mick?" I called out. "What on earth?"

He barely slowed, and it was obvious he planned to keep going until Alex grabbed his arm and yanked him to a stop. "What were you doing in Dolores Prescott's house?"

Mick's muscles bulged beneath his cut-off T-shirt as he struggled to pull away, but Alex held firm. He was inordinately strong for someone whose job it was to import wine.

Mick's face flushed with his efforts to get away. He was sweating, his eyes wide. "You don't understand. I didn't do it."

"Do what?" I asked, my sense of unease doubling by the second.

"Let me go. I didn't do it," Mick repeated. "I swear. I found her that way."

Without a further word, Alex marched Mick back to Dolores's cottage. The side door was swinging in the wind.

An icy-cold sensation took hold of me, and I shivered. Something terrible had happened. Jessie Rae's premonition flashed through my head. *The spirits. They're in turmoil. Everything churning, churning like the ocean. Waves crashing, falling. Something drops like a pin in the water but ripples...everything ripples.*

Alex pushed Mick back into the cottage even as he struggled, and I followed. We entered the dimly-lit hallway, the orange curtains drawn against daylight. I squinted.

It was worse than I'd feared.

On the floral-carpeted hallway was Dolores, face down, a knife protruding from her back.

"I found her like that," Mick whispered, his voice as hushed as if her ghost were listening.

"Is she...?" I asked Alex.

Without releasing Mick, he knelt over Dolores's prostrate body and pressed two fingers to her neck. He glanced up at me grimly. "Yes," he said. "She's dead."

I stared again at that dreadful, glinting knife before dashing out of the cottage, unable to breathe. I stood on the street inhaling the fresh air. Dolores was dead. I couldn't believe it.

I soon heard Alex and Mick arguing. I turned and saw the two men gesticulating wildly, just outside of the front door. Alex still had one hand on Mick's arm. His hold looked like a vise grip.

"You don't understand, mate," Mick was saying. "I didn't do it. And you can't go searching about in there. We can't touch anything. It's a crime scene. You'll see—there's none of my prints anywhere."

"How could you?" Alex snarled. "She was a defenseless pensioner."

"Wasn't me," Mick yelled. "How many times has a bloke got to say the same thing before it goes in? I'm no killer."

"Then what were you doing in her house?" Alex demanded, sounding like a terrifying headmaster.

I heard their conversation through a fog of consternation. There was no denying it—Mick appeared overwhelmingly guilty. We'd witnessed him literally running from a crime scene.

I was struck with guilt of my own. Hadn't I been the one to say that Mick could stay? Hadn't I given him a job and passed him on to Owen? A terrible gnawing sensation tortured my stomach. Was it my fault Dolores was dead? If I hadn't enabled Mick to stick around in Willow Waters, would Dolores still be alive?

I snapped back to life and called the police. I told them that they had to come immediately—a civilian was restraining a man I believed to be a murderer. Even as I said the words, they felt strange in my mouth, unwelcome interlopers.

The warmth of the last hour with Alex melted away, replaced by a disquiet that penetrated my very core. All that worry about Elizabeth Sanderson taking her revenge on Dolores, only for a complete stranger to beat her to it. And then I froze. Elizabeth had told Jessie Rae and me that she was going to shop on the internet for a revenge spell. We'd warned her not to—non-witches messing around with spells, especially ones that were malevolent, always produced unintended effects. Or came back around on the caster three times as strong.

I'd thought I had time to visit Elizabeth later and talk her out of it, but what if that decision had been foolish? Had Elizabeth found a spell and sent wicked vibrations into the universe? Had her mislaid revenge provoked Mick to murder a stranger? Had she caused Dolores's death? I desperately wanted to talk to my mom and get her take on this disaster.

My heart sank at how Char might react to this new chain of events. Mick had some kind of hold on her—even if it was only sharing a romantic past.

Char's muscular ex was still arguing and struggling with

Alex. To his credit, Alex was holding firm, in all ways. He must have a gym hidden somewhere in that gigantic castle of his.

I approached the two men with a steady gait. I focused on Mick, determined to get him to speak the truth. I needed to do it quickly before the police arrived and stopped me from interfering. I asked again, "What really happened here? Why were you in Dolores's cottage?"

Mick's eyes clouded over for a moment, as though trying to block the horror he'd witnessed. Or caused.

I thought he wouldn't answer, but then I heard the sound of a siren, and he turned to me as though I was his only hope in the world.

Rapidly, he began to speak. "I was s'posed to meet Owen at the pub. I was on my way, wasn't I? Noticed the old lady's patio door was ajar. It was like an open invitation. What can I say? See an open door—walk through it. It was quiet like. Thought she might be having a nap, or she'd gone out and left the door open. I figured she might have some valuables hanging around the place. Nothing too grand, just a few bits I could slip into my pockets. A smidgen of auntie's silver. Credit card on the sideboard. Cash under the mattress— you'd be amazed how many people still do that."

The siren was getting louder, coming closer. Mick swallowed hard. I hoped he wouldn't vomit before he got the full story out.

"I crept to the window at the back and had a peek through a crack in the curtains. Saw an empty sherry bottle and a couple of twenty-pound notes. Thought the old dear was sleeping off the sherry, and I'd nip in and help myself to the cash. Who'd notice forty quid missing? And I bet I need the money more than she does." He gulped. "Did."

Alex's fingers flexed as if he wanted to punch the man he was restraining, but held himself back. I saw him quiver with something like rage, and then he controlled himself.

Mick continued, "But I didn't get far. I went in the side entrance and there she was, face down, stabbed in the back. I ran out. I saw you guys. And now I'm in a pot of boiling water and the temperature's rising. Look. I have to get out of here." Mick's eyes were desperate. "I'm already wanted by the cops for a credit card fraud racket. That's why I came to see Char."

"So you lied to us," I said. "You didn't come here *for* Char. You came to hide from the police."

"Okay. I lied. So what? It's not that easy," was Mick's only defense. "I had no job. Char was gone. All I did was deliver some stuff in a van. I don't even know what was in the back, but it went wrong." He clamped his lips shut before saying more, as if suddenly reminded that the police were coming for him.

"You're already wanted by the police," I said, as though I needed to repeat the obvious. I was clearly still in shock.

"But I'm no murderer. I wanted valuables—not blood. I'm not that kind of guy. If they find me now, I'm done for. I'll get more than life in combination with this old lady's death. It'll be the end of me. You gotta let me go."

"I don't believe you," Alex said firmly. "I think Dolores caught you in the act, and you grabbed a knife and killed her. Maybe you didn't mean to, but knowing Dolores, she'd have set up a racket. Started screaming, threatened to call the police. And, as you've just told us, that's the last thing you want."

Mick shook his head, panic rising.

"It's not like that, I swear," he insisted. "Why would I? What could I possibly gain except trouble? And I got enough of that to last me a lifetime."

In a steely voice, Alex said, "Dolores's body was still warm when I checked for a pulse."

The harsh bleats of the siren tore through the air.

Mick tried to bolt again, but Alex grabbed him by both arms this time. And within seconds, four police officers arrived—two uniforms and then the two detectives, Rawlins and Evans, who'd visited me the other week. Mick gaped at them and then me, aghast. I could see he was trying, one last time, to appeal to the woman who'd let him into her home. But right now, I was ashamed of that woman. The uniformed officers rushed over and released Alex from his duty, detaining the struggling Mick.

Alex and I stood back and stared at the scene. Another murder marred the peace of our beautiful village.

CHAPTER 11

$\mathcal{T}$he paramedics arrived next. Sergeant Evans accompanied them into the cottage. DI Rawlins asked Alex and me, awkward participants in this drama, to step to one side and explain what had happened here. Quietly, I took the lead and told her that we'd simply been walking down the high street on the way to Roberto's café when we'd seen Mick running out of Dolores's cottage.

Rawlins was dressed head to toe in navy. She wore her gray hair short and had sharp eyes. As I spoke, she wrote in a notebook. I felt innately uncomfortable.

As you might already know, witches are naturally wary of the police. We just want to be left in peace to practice our magic. Historically, people have too often jumped to the wrong conclusions when it comes to women like me and my sisters, so we avoid any unnecessary attention.

But now here I was again, talking to the police. How I longed for the sleepier days of Willow Waters when getting a parking ticket was about the limit of lawbreaking. It was no coincidence that so many of us had chosen to live in such a quiet, drama-free place. Or at least that's what we'd thought we'd signed up for.

I also noticed that Alex was shifting from foot to foot. Was this where his reclusive nature came into play? Or was it something deeper than that? Only moments ago, Alex had been bravely holding on to Mick as that much younger muscled tear-away struggled hard. Now I sensed Alex wanted to be the one running, too.

"Mick came running from Dolores Prescott's cottage," I said, pointing at the open door. "When we caught him, he told us that she was dead. We took him back inside, and there she was—on the floor with a knife in her back." I blinked. It was going to take a long time for that image to fade in my mind. I explained that Alex had checked for a pulse and then we'd left.

"Do you corroborate this story?" Rawlins asked Alex.

"Absolutely," he said, his voice firm and unwavering. "Everything Ms. Bellefleur has told you is correct."

After the friendly familiarity of the afternoon, it was strange to hear Alex revert to calling me Ms. Bellefleur. But I supposed he was merely being formal with the detective.

Another siren exploded through the air and then the screeching of tires announced the arrival of backup. Four more police officers rushed from their cars, and the high street became saturated in flashing blue.

By now, everyone around the high street had emerged from their shops and homes, wondering what on earth was going on. You'll remember that Willow Waters is a sleepy village—we don't hear sirens very often, in fact, barely even a car's horn honking, and that's usually to get round a tour bus. So all this commotion was drawing a huge crowd. People piled onto the cobbled high street, mouths agog. Questions floated across the air.

"Has there been a break-in?"

"Who are they after?"

"What's happening to this village?"

"Why so many officers?"

"Is Dolores unwell?"

Oh, she was so much more than unwell, but I wasn't about to announce her death, so I stayed silent and tried to avoid the curious gazes of my neighbors.

The two new officers asked Alex and me to step back, and we retreated to the other side of the road. And then I saw Elizabeth. She was walking from Café Roberto toward the commotion with one of the women I recognized from choir practice.

"What's going on?" she murmured, staring wide-eyed at the ambulance outside Dolores's cottage, the lights still flashing but the siren now silent.

There was no longer any rush.

"Oh my goodness," she said, her hand going to her heart. "Has something happened to Dolores?" She came right up to me. "Peony, tell me she's okay."

I noticed her voice was shaking. What had she done?

I swallowed and glanced at Alex. His eyes were full of a sadness that I knew were also reflected in mine. I gave him a slight nod to say, *I'll do this.* "Oh, Elizabeth," I said, placing a gentle hand on her arm. "Dolores has been found dead."

"Dead?" she murmured. "Dead?"

Elizabeth's round eyes were disbelieving, and the most terrible look of pain crossed her face. "I don't understand," she half-whispered.

Her friend from the choir tightened her grip on Elizabeth's arm. Being in the choir, she must have also been a friend of Dolores, but she seemed more fixed on Elizabeth's reaction.

And then Elizabeth's chilling words came back to me once more. *I'm going to find a revenge spell on the internet instead.* But I also recalled the insistence on revenge for her ruined altar cloth. The way she tore up the apology note. The stamping on my beautiful flowers. I'd been so taken aback by the intensity of Elizabeth's reaction to her friend's apology. Could I have been wrong about Mick? Was it possible that Elizabeth had actually done this to Dolores all by herself?

She was near the crime scene, after all. Perhaps she'd slipped into the cottage, done the deed, and then swiftly made her way to Roberto's café. It was the perfect alibi. No one would notice the exact minute that she arrived at the always busy coffee shop, especially at this time of day. It was practically cake and coffee rush hour.

A murmur went around the crowd like a wave of disbelief. "Dolores is dead? What? Dolores is dead. Dolores is dead!"

I watched Elizabeth's face closely. It paled significantly as she took in the news. Her hands began to tremble, and then her tears came hard and fast, her voice a wail. The sound was awful, an echo of her performance at the choir rehearsal yesterday over the wine-stained embroidered cloth. But this time it wasn't about spilt wine. Her friend was dead.

The woman next to Elizabeth put an arm around her shoulders, but Elizabeth shrugged it off, and with an impressive speed, she rushed over to the two uniformed officers who were standing with Mick between them. I didn't know how these things worked, but it seemed they'd been given no instructions pertaining to the man caught at the scene. Or were the detectives waiting to question him right here while the body was still inside?

Elizabeth halted in front of the two officers. Between sobs, she gasped, "I need to go in there. And see her. I have to see my friend. Let me through, let me through."

"Ma'am, you must step back," the taller of the two said firmly. "This is a police crime scene, and we need to clear the area."

"Let me see her. I don't believe it. She was my best friend." She clutched the jacket of one of the officers.

"Madam, you need to control yourself. You're interfering with police affairs. It's a crime to prevent an officer from doing their job. Release me so I can do mine."

"My best friend. My oldest, closest friend." She reached for the other officer now, seizing his arm. "Oh, I can't bear it. We had a furious row, and I said terrible things. Now it's too late." At least, I think that's what she was trying to say. She was so hysterical her words were more like gasps.

I suspected the paramedics would soon be treating her.

I wondered if I should try to calm her with a spell, but I was worried she might fall and break a hip or something. I suspected the paramedics could treat her more efficiently. The scene was, frankly, chaos, and none of us standing around knew what to do.

As Elizabeth's wails grew louder, it was a terrible symphony of pain.

She collapsed, and both officers grabbed for her, laying hands on her this time.

All of us were focused on Elizabeth and in that moment,

that split second of confusion which ensued, Mick made a run for it.

The whole crowd seemed to freeze in unison, and the only thing moving was Mick's two feet. He was fast. An incredible amount of adrenaline must have been pumping through his body.

He shoved people out of the way, ran between two cottages, and disappeared from view.

"Stop!" yelled both of the officers.

One of them took the full weight of holding the unconscious Elizabeth, while the other took off after Mick. The four additional officers on the scene did so as well.

The vicar approached from out of the crowd and helped the officer lower Elizabeth carefully to the ground. "Can I get some medical assistance, please?" the vicar called in his commanding voice.

The officer, looking relieved to have a reason to get away, raced into the cottage to get a paramedic—and probably both detectives, too.

No doubt a lot of people would soon turn up to help.

The officers, who'd chased after Mick, changed direction and came running back for their cars. I could see their thinking, but they were losing valuable time.

I didn't think they'd have an easy time finding Mick. The young man's life was on the line, and he'd already slipped the law once. He had everything to run for and nothing to lose.

I shook my head as it dawned on me exactly how many hiding places Mick would have at his fingertips here in the Cotswolds. For those of you who've never visited this green part of England, it's full of villages, but between them are swathes of farmlands, woodlands, and permissive paths. The latter is a track where the landowner has granted permission allowing the public to walk or ride a horse across private lands.

There were so many places for a desperate person to hide.

And then I worried that Mick might head back to the farmhouse to pick up Char and drag her into this whole sorry mess. She had Frodo the truck (as she called it), after all. Maybe he would ask her to be his getaway driver. Did Char have the strength to refuse Mick? I had to hope so. I turned to Alex and told him I needed to get back to Char—I had to warn her and lock all the doors.

"Good idea," he said. "If I come with you, then could I borrow your car once you're home? I know the local area inside out, and I can hunt for Mick myself. Clearly, these officers are too rattled to do their job well."

I nodded, and we hurried back to my Range Rover. Thank goodness for Alex's clear head in a crisis.

I drove as fast as I could while staying safe. The last thing anyone needed was for me to crash my car. Char's beloved face flickered through my mind. I needed her to be safely in her bedroom. Or sitting with me and Hilary at the kitchen table. It felt like more than bad luck she was off work today.

Silence filled the space between Alex and me, both of us consumed with worry. It was a stark contrast to our lighter, more playful conversation earlier.

I pulled up at the farmhouse and jumped out. Alex took my place behind the wheel and said he'd be in touch. I nodded, fear mounting for Char, and ran to the front door.

CHAPTER 12

$\mathcal{A}$s I turned the key in the lock, Jessie Rae's voice called out my name.

"Mom?" I said. "What are you doing here? Where's Char?"

Jessie Rae looked agitated. Blue left her spot next to her and circled my ankles as I stepped inside. I picked her up, immediately grateful for the warm mass of ginger fur and the feeling of my power growing with my familiar in my arms.

"Char's in the garden with Norman.."

I let out a huge sigh of relief. The adrenaline coursing through my body had caused me to tense my shoulders unbearably, and now I let them relax.

"But the spirits are not calm," Jessie Rae added. "Not calm at all." She paused for a beat, then said, "Goodness, lassie, you look a sight. What's happened? Why are you here, my Peony? I'm here because the spirits are very upset." She clutched my hands and closed her eyes. "There's a new one, and it's a very angry destructive energy. Jessie Rae feels it's close by." She opened her eyes wide, the whites gleaming. "I felt the urge to come here and make sure my baby is safe. I felt its presence not long after you left the shop, and it's grown more angry and intense ever since."

I knew that feeling. It was how I'd felt about Char. We really were connected. "Oh, Mom. Something terrible *did* happen. But not to me." I locked the door behind me and walked with my mom to the kitchen and out the back doors —calling to Char, asking her to come inside right away.

Char was sitting on an old beach towel on the lawn. At my voice, she glanced up lazily from the book in her hands. She had on cut-off denim shorts, a short T-shirt, and heart-shaped red sunglasses. Norman perched beside her, dozing.

I repeated my request, more insistent now, scanning the garden, paranoid that at any moment Mick would come crashing through the bushes.

Norman jerked awake and said, "Do you mind? I'm sleeping here."

I didn't have time for Norman's nonsense today.

"Both of you. Inside. Now!"

Something passed between Char and me, and suddenly she leapt to her feet. "What is it?" she asked, running over. "I can feel it."

Norman swooped behind her, a protective presence at her back.

I ushered her, Norman, and my mom back inside. Then I locked the kitchen door—something I rarely did—and sat them down at the table. Blue jumped into Jessie Rae's lap, and she stroked my familiar behind her right ear.

"You're scaring me, Peony," Char said.

I hated what I had to tell her. But she was going to find out soon enough, and she had to be warned about her ex-boyfriend. I took a deep breath and recounted to everyone what had happened to Dolores today.

"A knife in the back?" Norman said, shocked. "That's cold. She wouldna seen it coming, at least."

Jessie Rae started to whisper under her breath and rocked back and forth on her chair. "Oh yes, they are angry, angry. Vile rage and silver glints."

Right now, I didn't have time for the spirits and their peculiar messages. I leaned across the table and took Char's hands in mind. "Char, we discovered Dolores because Alex and I were walking past her cottage when Mick came running out of her place."

Char sat up straight. "Mick? What was he doing there? He was working here today. I saw him. He only left to join Owen for a drink in the pub. Asked me to go along, but I wasn't in the mood."

"He claims he found Dolores like that. Dead, I mean."

"But why would he go into her house? He doesn't even know her."

I felt bad telling her, but Mick was not the reformed character we were all hoping for. "He said her door was open, and he saw an opportunity for a quick grab. Cards, cash, that kind of thing. Alex managed to restrain him, and I called the police, but there was a big scene with lots of confusion, and he managed to get away. He's on the run."

Char's pale skin grew even paler. "He promised me, all of us, he was trying to go straight. How could he do this?"

"I don't know." I felt betrayed too, so I couldn't imagine how Char must feel. "You mustn't talk to him or let him near you. He's obviously dangerous."

But Char shook her head at that, so the pink tips of her

hair flickered like newly polished fingernails. "Mick's no killer. You have to believe me. That man doesn't have it in him. He's an opportunist and a fool. But why did the idiot run? That just makes him look more guilty."

Suddenly, a loud banging on the back door made us all jump.

"Och, may the spirits save me," Jessie Rae moaned.

"I'll protect ya," Norman cried.

Char spun round. "Mick?"

But the face at the door belonged to Owen Jones.

I rose, putting a hand to my heart to try to steady its beat. Owen looked furious, so I figured he already knew about Mick and Dolores. News traveled fast round here.

But as I invited him in, Owen asked if we'd seen Mick— he'd stood him up at the pub. They'd agreed to meet at The Mermaid after they'd finished the first part of my stone path. Owen went home to shower, but Mick said he wouldn't bother and would head straight there. "Been sitting there on my tod for almost forty-five minutes," he grumbled in his Yorkshire accent. "I mean, you try and give a young lad a break, and then this is how he repays you?"

I locked the door behind Owen, my gaze furtively darting around the garden, searching for any sign of someone watching.

"Owen," Char said quietly, standing up from her chair. "It's not like that at all. Peony, tell him what's happened."

As I quickly relayed the afternoon's events at Dolores's cottage, he shook his head in sorrow. "What an idiot," he said.

"That's what I said," Char replied. Then she put her hands over her eyes. "It's all my fault. We never should have let him stay in Willow Waters."

"On the run from the law and breaking and entering?" Owen continued. He thumped his fist against the kitchen cabinet. "I left that guy alone for one minute and look what he's got himself involved in. Trouble attracts trouble."

I told Owen to sit, and I went to put the kettle on. Herbal tea would help calm everyone's nerves. Though maybe a whiskey was more in order.

I made a big pot of rosehip tea and passed round the mugs. But Owen declined. I noticed now that he'd put on a clean plaid shirt for the pub and his cheeks smelled of cologne.

"I feel responsible for not watching him closely enough," Owen said. "I'm going to join the manhunt. Maybe if I find him first, I can convince him to turn himself in. The young fool."

The three of us tried to persuade him otherwise—the police were on the case and Alex was already driving around in my car, but Owen was insistent and he left, warning us to keep the doors locked in case Mick *was* stupid enough to come back here.

I felt doubly bad with Owen getting involved. He'd taken Mick in as a favor to me, which by extension was a favor to Char. Owen had had enough trouble over at Lemmington House, and now he was being dragged into another murder investigation. I took a sip of my tea and tried to let the hot floral liquid calm me down.

Char paced the kitchen with Norman on her shoulder. "Stupid Mickey, so stupid. He's his own worst enemy, that man. Always has been, always will be."

"Stupid Mickey, stupid Mickey, what a silly boy," Norman sang happily.

"For once, Normie, I agree," Char said, still frowning.

"Char," I said, trying to keep my tone soothing, "please sit. There's nothing we can do."

Char kept pacing. "He's stupid, but not a killer. That's one thing that man is not. There's no way Mick has that in him. I know." Her gaze darted to me. "Peony, should we—?"

But before she could continue, I interrupted. "No, it's no use, Char. There's already enough people hunting for Mick."

Char stuck out her bottom lip. "But those people aren't witches. And they don't know Mick the way I do. He might listen to me. I'm taking Frodo out for a spin. Alone if I have to. Nothing you can say will stop me."

Sometimes, living with Char was like having my own petulant teenager. She never listened to reason, was determined to go her own way *in* her own way. And I was powerless. I know, I know, a witch like me powerless? But yes, I couldn't bring myself to stamp out her light, or even bottle it up for her own safety. She was going to have to learn the hard way sometimes, and it was up to me as her protective big sister to allow that to happen.

"I'm going with you. You don't have enough control over your powers yet to try to calm Mick. He might steal the truck and use it to get away. Plus, that truck means too much to both of us for anything bad to happen to it."

"Not *it* but *him*," Char corrected. "Frodo."

I had to laugh. "Frodo," I repeated.

"Fine," Char said, finally shrugging. "Two witches are better than one, anyway."

I turned to my mom and asked her to guard over the house and our familiars. "No convening with the spirits, okay? I need you in this realm only. You have to stay alert.

Hilary will be home soon, and you need to protect her as well."

"Och, lassie, you know you can rely on me. Blue and I will stand guard. I'll put a good protection spell around the house, don't you worry. That young man won't get past us."

"And me!" Norman whined. "Why is everyone always forgetting about me? I'm very fierce." He made an attempt at a growl.

Char rolled her eyes. "See you, Normie. Be a good dog."

As we left, I triple-checked that the front door had locked behind us—sadly, not something I normally had to worry about. And then Char and I climbed into the old truck. She got Frodo's engine revving, and we drove out. I was pleased that she was driving like a sensible woman and not a maniac. The truck was built for might, not speed, and putting us into a ditch would help no one.

Soon we were powering down the road. Char's expression was set, determined.

"Keep your cool," I warned. "Don't let your anger or frustration or worry get the better of you, otherwise fire will start shooting out your fingertips. The last thing we need is to have to call out the fire department. I've had enough of Willow Waters' emergency services for one day."

Char only grunted in response, but I could tell she didn't want to set fire to Frodo. She flexed her fingers and took a slow, calming breath.

"That's better," I said, feeling her edges smooth.

But then it occurred to me that we had no plan.

It must have occurred to Char as well because she asked, "Do you think he might have gone back to Owen's cottage? He'd want his stuff."

"It would be a dumb move," I said, "as that would be the first place Owen would check. The police too, if they've done their homework on Mick."

"No one but us knows Mick's staying here, remember?" Char said.

"We hoped to keep his whereabouts secret, but who knows in this village? Even so, I think we're better off looking in the fields, or parking up and taking the woodland paths. If I was on the run, I'd go to nature and hope she'd shield me for the night until I figured things out."

Char snorted. "Mick's a motorcycle head. He's hardly going to be meditating under a tree seeking guidance."

"Where's his motorcycle?"

She shrugged. "Parked at Owen's cottage, I guess."

"Then let's start there."

"Owen will already have checked. And if he got there first, Mick's already taking the back roads, hoping to evade capture."

"I hope Owen gets to him and talks him into surrendering."

"If that boy has a shred of common sense in him, then that's what he'll do." Char didn't sound convinced about that shred.

"Let's take the road by the fields."

Char drove more slowly now. We stayed silent, both of us straining our necks to catch sight of Mick's hulk or a flash of his tattoos among the green. I kept warning Char to keep her eyes on the road. Empty as it was, we had to keep our wits about us.

She'd obey the command, staring ahead again—before

seconds later swiveling to look left and right again. "It's no good," she said finally. "I don't think he's here."

I could tell Char was feeling demoralized. I urged her not to give up hope. Mick would be found sooner or later.

"Isn't there, like, a finding spell we can cast?" she asked.

"Yes," I admitted. "But we'd need an item which belonged to Mick to cast it. Do you have one?"

Char shook her head. "I burned everything to do with Mick after he dumped me. His T-shirt that I used to sleep in. The oil rag I borrowed and never gave back. Every photo. I had to cleanse my entire aura of his being."

Before we reached the turn to Lemmington House, a truck came toward us, which I recognized as the one Owen drove. We slowed and then stopped side by side. I had the window open, and so did Owen.

"What are you two doing out?" He demanded before I could ask if he'd found anything. "I told you to stay put."

I didn't care for his tone, but I could see him staring past me to Char, sitting grimly behind the wheel and knew that it was his care for her causing him to sound so bossy. "Char knows Mick best. Don't worry." I waved my cell phone. "We'll call for help if we sight him."

"Well, if you're looking for his motorcycle, he hasn't taken it." Owen appeared grimly satisfied. "And he won't. I've locked it away in my garage. Even if he thinks to look there, it's beyond his feeble powers to break the electronic lock system."

"Good thinking," I said. "So, without wheels, he's still in the area."

"Unless he's stolen a car," Owen reminded me. "Now you two stay safe." Then he nodded and drove on.

Char and I remained rooted to the spot for a minute. Presumably both wondering what to do next.

Finally, I said, "Let's drive to the woodland. It's darker. Maybe he's thinking of holing up in there for the night rather than crossing the fields. He any good at climbing trees?"

Char nodded glumly and took the next sharp left. "Probably. He's scaled enough walls in his life."

The windows were wound down and as we approached the wood, she began to call Mick's name. Only the birds replied, chirping louder and more insistently—a pretty song, but one which couldn't penetrate our worry. The afternoon warmth had faded, and the sky's light was changing from vivid to pale. I shivered, but it wasn't from the cold.

"Wait," Char said, slowing down to barely a crawl. "Do you feel that?"

"I think so. The temperature changed."

"I can feel anguish. I think he's nearby."

I was struck by how in tune Char had become with her intuition. And then I felt something else. The sensation of being watched. But there was nothing around us but woodland. "Pull over," I said quietly.

Char obeyed. She switched off the engine. Nothing but birdsong, yet the scene was far from idyllic. We were purposefully chasing a suspected murderer instead of being safely at home in the farmhouse with all the doors locked. Yes, I know our combined powers were great protection, but it didn't mean I'd lost all sense of my own mortality. I just hoped that when the time came, we'd be strong enough together to face anything.

And then a scream of pain cut through the air. I felt like

we were being attacked. I stretched out my arms to let my power surge through me.

Char grabbed my fingertips and pulled them down. "It's Mick!" she said. "That's him screaming." Her seatbelt clicked, and she leapt out of the truck.

I followed, adrenaline coursing through me as I mentally prepared a holding spell to restrain Mick. With Char by my side, I'd have enough power to carry us through.

We crashed through the bushes and then the sound of cursing rose above the blood pumping in my veins. Wow, could that man's swearing color the air. What was going on? Had he stumbled into an illegal badger trap?

"Over there," Char said, and then shouted, "Mick! Mick, it's me!"

I followed her gaze, and in a small clearing I saw him, hunched over and clutching his leg.

He was wounded. Badly enough that he couldn't run when he saw us approaching.

I glanced around, trying to get back my breath and, out of the corner of my eye, caught the hindquarters of a wolf running away. I gasped. I knew immediately that it was the same wolf with a brown hide and startling gray-blue eyes that I'd seen the other week. He disappeared from sight.

Mick was howling in pain, still doubled over. A restraining spell wasn't going to be necessary—he was already completely incapacitated. The wolf had done the work for us.

"It bit me," he yelled as Char fell to her knees by his side.

Although Mick couldn't harm her in this state, I was still on high alert. I glanced back at where the wolf had disappeared.

"What happened?" Char asked. There was blood everywhere.

"It was the fiercest dog I've ever seen. Sharp, wild eyes, huge brown body, teeth like shards of glass, I tell ya. I said, 'Nice doggy, good doggy,' but it just came for me. It pounced on me, knocked me over, and then bit my leg. Shaking me from side to side like I was a juicy bone."

"Be glad he didn't go for your throat," I said.

Char helped Mick to his feet. He yelled with pain, but I could see the wound wasn't too bad.

"Will he need a tetanus shot? Rabies?" she asked me as I took Mick's other side and we helped him hobble toward the truck.

"I'm not sure. But we'll take him to the hospital and let them decide."

"Dog should be shot," Mick muttered.

And good luck with that. Mick had described the animal perfectly, except he was wrong about his eyes. They were sharp, yes, but not wild. Those eyes were all-seeing and completely in control.

"Let's get you to the hospital," Char said. "They'll sort you out."

Mick shook his head. "No, no, I've got to keep going. I didn't kill that old lady. I swear it on every bone in my body. Even this one with the teeth marks on it. You've got to help me. Hide me. Please." Mick's voice was thick with desperation, and despite the evidence against him, I did wonder if he was telling the truth.

"If you're innocent," I said, "then you've got nothing to worry about. You can't outrun the police forever. You have to pay your dues for the crime you have actually committed. If they send you down for driving the getaway car, then that'll only be what was coming to you, anyway."

Mick sent Char an appealing look. But she turned her head away.

It was hard to tell what Char was feeling. All I knew was that she was holding it together...and she was strong as anything. Between us, we guided a hobbling Mick back to the truck.

We put him in the cab of the truck between us, and I gave Char directions to the nearest hospital. While she drove, it was up to me to call the police for the second time today. I dialed 999 and, taking a deep breath, I told the person on the other end of the phone who I was, that we'd found Mick, and he was injured.

After a set of questions, I suggested she get hold of DI Rawlins or Sergeant Evans and tell them which hospital we were heading for.

The operator told me that only if we felt safe, should we continue driving Mick to the nearest hospital. The police would be waiting for us there. They'd arrest and interview Mick after he'd been treated.

Mick sat wedged between us, miserable. "I didn't kill anyone, Char. You have to believe me. I was only going to see if she had any money or valuables lying around and be out of there on the fly to meet Owen at the pub."

"This is one time you should have just gone straight to the pub, Mick," she said firmly, a disappointed expression pinching her face. "You promised me you'd changed."

"Yeah, I know. I'm sorry about that, babe." And the sad thing was, I believed him.

CHAPTER 13

*I*t was hard to concentrate at work the next day. Images of the wolf flashed through my mind. Startling gray-blue eyes penetrating mine. At the hospital, Mick had described the dog to the incredulous staff, and I'd watched as he was wheeled away. The police arrived and said they'd come to take statements from us both tomorrow after they'd had a chance to interview Mick.

We returned home, exhausted. Char was shaken up and went to bed early.

I'd asked Norman to keep an eye on her during the night. "Time to earn your familiar stripes," I'd said, and for once, Norman quit playing the fool and took his job seriously.

Maybe too seriously.

He'd been acting peculiar all morning, sitting solemnly inside the window of Bewitching Blooms, watching the high street. At first, I'd thought he was looking out for Char. But his gaze was too unfocused. No wisecracks. No demands for food. He was eerily quiet.

"Come on now, you're spooking me," I said, trying to

cajole him from whatever funk had taken hold. "That last customer had a piece of toilet roll stuck to her shoe the whole time she was choosing those tulips. And no wisecrack from you? Was it too easy or something? Tell me what's up."

Norman preened himself and then hung his head. "Dolores wasn't much, but I lived with her. Can't believe she's gone."

It was the last thing I was expecting Norman to say. Maybe my witchy intuition didn't extend to parrots. I told him I was sorry; it hadn't occurred to me that he might be fond of his previous person. I couldn't say owner, as I didn't think anyone could own Norman. He was his own bird. He'd seemed pretty keen to get away from Dolores and attach himself to Char, and that's exactly what had happened. He used those colorful wings to steer his own destiny.

"She wasn't much," he said. "But she looked after me when I was between witches. Maybe if I'd been with her, I could have saved her. Pooped in that little schmuck's eyes so he couldn't see to kill her."

A laugh was surprised out of me on a day when I hadn't expected to laugh. A killer swayed from his mission by parrot poop? Now that would be a headline for *Willowers Weekly*. Maybe all that target practice had been for a reason. But Norman's guilt was almost more than I could stand. Between Char's certainty, and my own gut instinct, I wasn't convinced that Mick *did* kill Dolores. Even with the pain of his wounded leg, Mick had stuck to his story, desperate to convince us of his innocence. I sensed he was telling the truth. I shared my feelings with Norman, who was pretty skeptical. I feared that was how the police would see things, too. It would be so easy to put Dolores's death down to Mick and his past mistakes. But maybe Norman could help me.

"Do you know who else might have had it in for Dolores?" I asked. "You must have seen her visitors, heard her arguments."

He made a parrot sound of disbelief and flapped his wings. "Who didn't have it in for Dolores? She wasn't exactly sweet as sugar, was she, Cookie? But she was my keeper all the same." He turned forlornly back to the window.

So much for Norman's help.

"No one in particular stands out?"

"The blonde tootsie had a fight with Dolores. I wasn't living there anymore, but I was in her cherry tree checking out my old 'hood."

"Blonde tootsie? You mean Elizabeth Sanderson?"

He shook his colorful head. "The fancy piece from the big house. She said—" And here he put on a posh accent that sounded exactly like Gillian Fairfax. *"I'm warning you, if you don't stop making my life hell, you'll be very sorry."*

Wow. That did sound nasty. I knew Gillian Fairfax had blamed Dolores for how hard she was having to try to fit into Willow Waters, but had she been angry enough to kill?

WEDNESDAY WAS Imogen's day off, and I flipped the 'back in five' sign and told Norman I was running out for coffee. With Dolores's cottage a crime scene, the high street was busier than usual. Techs were coming and going, ducking under the tape which sectioned off her cottage from the rest of the street. It was a sorry sight. Like something from a movie, not real life. I couldn't believe Dolores was gone.

In addition to getting coffee, I'd taken a break to find something to tempt Norman's appetite and put a wisecrack back in his speech.

Happy Tails pet shop was a family-run store next to Amanda's bakery on the other end of the high street. It stocked an array of essentials, toys, and treats for all pets, and I went there to buy Blue's food and litter. I'd also bought her a scratching post that she refused to use and three toys in the shapes of a tomato, carrot, and onion, which she also rolled her feline eyes at. There was an organic section, of course, because this was the Cotswolds, after all, so I figured I could find something tempting for Normie.

I couldn't bring back Dolores, but maybe I could ease her ex-parrot's depression.

The bell dinged as I walked in. Kevin, the owner's teenage son, was behind the counter and I realized it must be half term for the schools and colleges. He recognized me and waved hello before returning his attention to his book. I went to the bird section and found the sesame sticks that I knew Normie liked, as well as dried banana chips that I thought he might enjoy. Kevin rang up my order and then wrapped the packages in pink tissue paper. I told him Norman was struggling to accept Dolores's death.

Kevin nodded with great understanding. "Give Norman my best. He can come here and visit with me if he's feeling upset. So long as my parents don't see him."

"Don't tell me Norman's caused trouble here as well," I said, exasperated. Had the pesky parrot played target practice at Happy Tails as well?

But Kevin assured me the trouble wasn't Norman's fault. "Anyone who comes in for a pet expects them to be as smart as Norman." He shook his head. "Bad for business."

Of course, I needed some treats of my own, so I headed to Roberto's for a very necessary caffeine infusion. It was packed, every table taken and covered with coffee cups and plates of cake.

Poor Char appeared harried—and worried. She looked younger, more vulnerable, her hair in a messy knot on the top of her head. She was wearing a soft white oversized T-shirt which hung in folds over black leggings. Long silver hoops dangled from her ears and swished each time she turned from the coffee machine to a customer.

I joined the queue and tried to drown out the conversations speculating about the murder. It was impossible not to be surprised at how people were already singing Dolores's praises when I knew how disliked she'd been in life.

"She did such a lot for the community," one woman was saying to her friends.

"Oh yes, the WI would have been lost without her. She was always thinking about others."

"All those hours she volunteered at the church. The vicar will probably devote the entire sermon to her," said another.

"Dolores was my friend for decades," another voice chimed in. Then sighed. "I'm going to miss her wonderful personality."

"And such a sense of humor."

"I can't believe I won't see her again."

"Of course, she could be firm. Used to chase the cats out of her garden with a broom," one said. There was a pause. "But she loved birds."

"Do you remember when she had a parrot?" another woman said. "And how it talked. It was quite a mimic too."

In a way, it was nice that no one was speaking ill of Dolores, but boy, did Willowers have selective memories.

"Terrible what happened. A lone murderer, they're saying. A criminal who found himself in Willow Waters and thought he'd steal from us. I'm sure she fought him off. Dolores would have done that. And he killed her. Terrible thing."

So people were convinced Mick had killed Dolores. I couldn't be sure that he hadn't done it, but I felt there were other possibilities, all of which meant there was a murderer still on the loose. Not that I was afraid, but I was certainly more on the side of staying alert and inquisitive. My nerves were still wired from the whole scene yesterday, but I especially couldn't forget my terrible worry for Char as Alex and I raced home to make sure Mick hadn't got to her first. My big-sister vibes were in overdrive.

I was concerned for Char in general. She'd had a difficult childhood and thought she'd escaped her past and started afresh when she came to Willow Waters. Now her past was messing with her present. I mean, how much more messy could it get being attached to someone arrested for murder? Obviously, she was tough—a tough cookie, as Normie would say. But that didn't mean she couldn't be hurt. I watched as Char frothed milk for a cappuccino. I wished I could give her a hug. It was hard to let her know how much I cared without embarrassing her.

When it was my turn to order, I got a tired smile from Char. We had a hurried conversation where she assured me she was coping, and it was better to be at work listening to the whole town gossip about her ex than to sit at home worrying.

She passed me my usual coffee plus a *pastel de nata*. I had a soft spot (probably quite literally) for those little Portuguese custard tarts, and I knew it would be the perfect thing to brighten my morning. Who doesn't love a sugar rush, after all?

The door jangled, and I checked the time. Eleven a.m. and Alex was right on time for his usual espresso. He was back in his usual slacks and starched white shirt, his shoes so polished they gleamed like wet stones. I instinctively straightened and smoothed the white cotton sundress I'd donned that morning for a change. Yes, I was still wearing sneakers, but I'd woken in a mood to feel feminine. Now I was glad I'd followed my instincts. Not that I cared what Alex thought, of course, but—

"Peony," he said, putting a hand on my shoulder. "I was hoping to find you here. I heard you caught Mick!"

I nodded yes, pleased to see him looking more rested than yesterday.

"You had better luck than I did tracking him down," he continued.

But did I? I shot him a skeptical glance.

"I'm glad no harm came to you or Char."

"We make a pretty formidable team," I said, smiling. We had the power of two (relatively) young witches, after all. I realized I'd calmed considerably. Any worry I was feeling about Willow Waters and murderers paled when Alex was around. It was a power I wasn't used to experiencing from other people.

"And how are the preparations for Monsieur Gagneux

going?" I asked, desperate for talk of anything but murder. "Are you getting the castle in order?"

He nodded grimly. "The company I hired arrived this morning. The team usually works on movie sets and preparing high-end houses for sale. They're polishing the floors, moving in enough furniture to fill three castles, unrolling rugs, and—I had to get out of there." He ran a hand through his dark hair as embarrassment flashed across his face. It made his gray-blue eyes appear lighter and more innocent. "To be honest, it's a bit much having all those people milling around the house with their bright smiles and all those questions. I'm not used to the company."

Well, that was the understatement of the year. No one I knew had been inside his castle, and now it was full of people used to working in showbiz and real estate. It would be a huge adjustment for anybody, let alone Alex, the man who notoriously kept himself behind closed doors.

I told Alex I had put in a rapid order for the tuberose and jasmine plants and was expecting the delivery tomorrow. "Plenty of time to get it all ready before dinner on Friday. I promise that the arrangements are going to be out of this world." I was pretty pleased with myself, pulling in favors to get the exotic plants in time and promising to pay Imogen overtime.

But Alex's brow was still furrowed.

"What is it?" I asked softly.

"I have another problem. Monsieur Gagneux is bringing his wife." He looked incredibly uncomfortable. "I'd assumed we'd have a business dinner, the two of us, but he seems to mix business with pleasure." He sounded put out.

"Oh well, surely that will make things easier? Less intense?"

Alex cleared his throat. "I thought it might make things a tinge uneven, numbers wise." He lowered his voice. "Well, actually, I was wondering if you'd consider being my fourth dinner guest? As a favor."

I blinked. Did Alex just invite me to dinner? At the castle? With his fancy-pants French client? Maybe I was a last-minute desperation invite, but I still felt flattered. Obviously, I don't get out much.

"How lovely," I said finally. "Of course. I'd love to come."

While Alex wasn't exactly asking me for a date, I was pleased he saw us as such good friends. Besides, I was definitely curious about Alex. He was easy on the eyes, for sure, but I was also certain there was more to him than met the eye, if you follow my drift. And it would be nice to have someone other than Hilary or my mom to cook dinner. I couldn't even remember the last time a man had cooked for me.

He sighed as if relieved. "You've no idea how much this means. I only hope you won't be dreadfully bored."

I was pretty sure I wouldn't be.

CHAPTER 14

I returned to Bewitching Blooms with a cappuccino, Normie's treats, and a spring in my step. I was glad it was Imogen's day off. I was sure that I had a girlish flush to my cheeks, and I couldn't bear to be teased by a twenty-something. Was I crushing on Alex? Or was I simply flattered by his attention? It was so long since I'd had any romantic inclination that I barely even remembered how it felt.

But any rush of pleasure I had disappeared as I spotted DI Rawlins and Sergeant Evans waiting outside my shop door. They both wore serious expressions. I let out my breath and then apologized for keeping them waiting and for not being able to shake hands. Rawlins cast a shrewd brown eye over my coffee and parrot treats and then wrinkled her nose ever so slightly.

I explained I had a depressed parrot in the store and then trailed off. Rawlins barely batted an eyelash. I guessed she had seen and heard it all before. No parrot story was going to rattle her cool.

I let the detectives inside and hoped to keep Normie quiet with an offering of banana chips. He perked right up when he saw the treats, and I wondered for a second if I'd been played by a parrot. Probably.

"These are for being good, Normie," I whispered. "No asides, no sarcastic comments. This is the police, and it's not a joke. Can you make me a promise?"

"Pinky swear, pinky swear," he bleated.

Both detectives stared in our direction. Evans looked amused. Rawlins less so.

"Right with you," I said, and handed Norman more banana chips.

He was delighted and retreated to the corner to munch.

Needless to say, the detectives probably thought I was a little kooky, but I suspect you might think that, too.

I invited Rawlins and Evans to take a seat and asked if they'd like some coffee, too. "If I'd known you were here, I would have picked you up something from Roberto's. He does the most amazing flat white and the pistachio loaf cake is to die for." I stopped abruptly.

Rawlins was contemplating me as if I were crazed. I'd better stop the nervous chatter before she petitioned to arrest me.

They declined my offer of coffee, so I sat down facing them, feeling as if I were back in seventh grade. They were both wearing a slightly modified version of the same outfits they had each time I'd seen them. Rawlins was wearing head to toe navy, but this time had paired her pantsuit with a pale-blue shirt. Evans was wearing a light-gray shirt that matched the hair of his boss, lazily tucked into the waistband of his pants. His sleeves were casually rolled up and his collar unbuttoned.

Rawlins took out a notepad and told me that Mick had been formally charged with murder.

"Okay," I replied. "I understand." I wasn't convinced they had the right man, but I also wasn't convinced they didn't.

They wanted to know exactly what I'd seen outside Dolores's cottage, and how I'd managed to find Mick after he escaped, in greater detail. I knew that it was Mick they were after, but again I couldn't help feeling put on the spot. I took a sip of my coffee and thought longingly of the *pastel de nata* waiting in its crisp paper bag. I'd much rather stuff my face with Portuguese pastry than answer these questions.

The first part was easy. I explained that I had been walking with Alex (quickly correcting myself to say Baron of Fitzlupin and then Lord Fitzlupin and then back to Alexander Stanford) when we saw Mick rushing out from Dolores's cottage.

I related everything that had happened right up to entering the cottage. "That's when we saw Dolores on the floor." I gulped as the image of the dead woman rose in front of me yet again. "She had been stabbed in the back."

Rawlins didn't consult her notes, just regarded me steadily, which made me feel incredibly guilty and nervous. "Michael Fry claims he wasn't in Willow Waters on the run from the authorities, but was working. For you."

Michael Fry? Oh, that must be Mick's name. And there went my good intentions, getting me in trouble. Again.

I nodded. Buying time. I could only nod for so long. Finally, I said, "He was a friend of a friend and pursuing work. I hired him to do some gardening."

There was a pause. I didn't fill it.

Finally, she asked, "A friend of a friend? Who's the friend?"

Crap. I hadn't wanted to bring Char into this, but I couldn't find a way out without lying, and I wasn't going to lie to the authorities.

"He's a friend of my..." I paused for a moment, wondering how to describe Char. Young witch protégé-slash-runaway wasn't going to cut it. "My lodger."

"I see," Rawlins said.

"Mick was laying a stone path in my garden. Doing an okay job, too. It was only casual labor for a few days."

"Did you see him act with violence in any way? Did he threaten you or steal from you?"

"No." Then I realized I hadn't actually searched the whole house. "I don't think so. I mean, not violence or threat. He definitely didn't do that, but I didn't scour the house to check if anything was missing." Then I felt I should say something in Mick's defense. "I know he's a thief, but I really don't think he's a murderer."

Rawlins raised her eyebrows and, with a voice dripping with sarcasm like honey from a spoon, asked, "And what, in your experience, does a murderer look like?"

Ouch. "It's not so much about looks, but more of a feeling."

"Let's just keep to facts, shall we?"

It took all my witchy might not to roll my eyes. I knew that the police needed to operate on black and white facts, but I also knew that wasn't how the world worked.

Feelings, intuition, sixth senses—that's how I got to the bottom of things, how I scraped through the murk and the mystery of the world. And I trusted my instincts implicitly. But of course, I could say none of this to either Rawlins or Evans—the latter of whom was suspiciously quiet. I glanced at him and wondered if he was more in tune with the complex workings of the world. Could I have an ally in Evans?

"And can you tell us more about how you discovered where Mr. Fry was hiding?"

I explained that Char and I had gone searching for him as we were hoping to help him turn himself in. "We only found Mick because of his terrible howling. He was in a lot of pain. We followed the sound, and that's when I rang the police." I couldn't mention a wolf was loose, so I said, "He'd been bitten by a dog."

"Yes," Rawlins said.

For a moment, I panicked—did that make it sound like Char was in on Mick's racket?

"Mr. Fry fled the scene of a murder, then escaped police custody. Yet you're unconvinced Mr. Fry is a murderer," Rawlins said. When she put it like that, Char and I sounded like a pair of fools tricked by a pretty face and a hot bod. I could tell that's what they were thinking.

"More bicep than brain," Normie suddenly chirped. "Not cunning enough to kill."

"Even your parrot has an opinion on the murder," Evans said, blinking as if slightly stunned.

I was relieved as I watched them go. But not so pleased with Norman. "You said you'd keep quiet."

"Hey, where's the gratitude? I got rid of the fuzz, didn't I? I don't want you going to jail, Cookie. You give me good treats."

Maybe it was the banana chips, maybe it was the way he

took credit for getting rid of the detectives, but Norman perked right up.

I admit I was glad to see them go, and determined to keep my head down for the rest of the day and think only about flowers. And dresses. I couldn't forget about dresses, because what on earth was I going to wear for Alex's fancy dinner in two days' time?

There was only one decent boutique in town, and I didn't want to arouse gossip by running in to buy something for dinner with Lord Fitzlupin. I also didn't have time to go to London. Did I have anything suitable in my closet? It had been so long since I'd dressed up that I seriously doubted it.

I NEEDN'T HAVE WORRIED. Later that evening, Hilary and Jessie Rae and even Char crowded around me, cooing like teenagers, as I told them about my invitation to the Fitzlupin Castle. No one was interested in making dinner.

Instead, they each gave their unsolicited advice as to what I should wear and how I should do my hair. I had an offer of kaftans and bangles from my mom, a red cocktail dress from Hilary along with her pearl necklace and matching earrings, and Char thought it appropriate to bring out a magenta-colored body-con dress that I could never imagine even Char wearing, let alone me. Even Norman swooped down with his brightest tail feather that had fallen out earlier and suggested I wear it as a brooch. I was touched, but decided to see what was in my own closet first.

"You're a beautiful woman when you put in the effort, my

darling," Jessie Rae said. "What should she do with all that bonny dark hair?" she asked in a raised voice.

I wasn't sure if she was consulting Hilary and Char or the spirits. With my luck, it was the latter, and I'd end up going to dinner looking like an 1890s Gibson girl.

"No offense, Peony, but you're not exactly creative with your locks. It's either down or in a ponytail. I mean, it's not very imaginative, is it?" She tossed her own red ringlets and turned to Char. "Are you on that Tick-Clock? Maybe we could find her a hair tutorial to follow."

"I'll be all right, thanks," I insisted. "Is anyone making dinner?"

Hilary said she'd been reading that we should all move to a plant-based diet to save the planet, so she was going to roast cauliflower and serve it with quinoa and vegetables. "I printed an excellent recipe off the internet," she said, pausing to read the printout she'd just mentioned. Hilary liked to follow an exact recipe, while Mom and I were more likely to cook by inspiration. Dinners were always interesting. "Oh dear," Hilary said. "I can't make it tonight. We don't have any tahini." She read on. "Or lemon grass."

It was pointless to suggest substitutions to Hilary. So that was that.

"For what it's worth," Char said, "I think your hair should be down and brushed a hundred times with a flat-paddle brush. It'll be soft and gleaming that way. You could have some of my hair mask. It smells like strawberries."

I groaned. "Is anybody listening to me? We're going to starve to death this way."

I strode over to the fridge and took a long look inside. If no one was going to help, then I'd make the lentil stew no one liked. I began to pull out tomatoes, carrots, and celery. "Could you grab me an onion?" I asked my mom.

But instead of helping, Jessie Rae suggested Princess Leia style braids, while Hilary chimed in saying I should attempt a French chignon. She hinted that I watch a YouTube tutorial and learn how best to sweep my dark locks into something European-looking and fancy.

All their suggestions were actually helpful, but maybe not in the way they intended. I vowed then and there to look and act completely natural. A simple dress, simple make-up, and comfortable shoes. I didn't need to dress up as anything other than who I was. And, in my humble opinion, Peony Bellefleur was a pretty good option.

I must have something tucked away from when Jeremy and I had been a social couple. Perhaps it would be a few years old, but did a little black dress ever go out of style?

CHAPTER 15

*W*hen Thursday arrived, a flurry of orders came into the shop. There was a big fortieth birthday party at the weekend and the warm weather was luring an even larger crowd of holidaymakers to our lovely village. Plus, there was my usual order for The Tudor Rose. It was great news for Bewitching Blooms, even if I was having trouble keeping my mind in the game.

I was also getting a few orders for Dolores's funeral, which had been scheduled for next Tuesday. I'll be honest with you—it wasn't many orders. The WI said they were providing posies from their gardens. I couldn't help but feel it was all out of duty, not friendship. Dolores had rubbed too many people the wrong way.

And it seemed that everyone had sided with Elizabeth Sanderson, but I had my suspicions about Dolores's so-called best friend, too. She'd been so distraught over Dolores's death that I had to wonder whether she'd somehow played a hand in it. Could she have confronted her old friend in the fury I'd witnessed at Mom's shop? Had she been enraged enough to kill? The whole thing left me feeling subdued.

"Do you think there'll be much of a turnout for the funeral?" I asked Imogen, as she pruned a rose for one of the big arrangements for Alex's dinner.

She was as excited as I was about the commission and had devoured my photos of the interior of Fitzlupin Castle. I'd given them to her for perspective and dimensions of the rooms, but I knew she was also enjoying this sneak peek into the secret world of the baron.

"He's definitely a bachelor," she said, staring at a photo of the drawing room. "And is he skateboarding on those floors? Look at the state of them."

I agreed they were in dire need of refinishing. I hoped the staging company could perform a miracle by tomorrow night.

Imogen was frowning in concentration, her nose wrinkling. "A turnout for Dolores's funeral? Yes, for sure. But not because people want to pay their respects per se. More like they can't be seen *not* turning up. The WI are doing most of the flowers from duty, not affection." She shrugged. "I'll be going and so will my parents and all their friends, and none of us could stand the woman." She paused. "May she rest in peace."

"Hmm, that's exactly what I was thinking." I understood duty and doing the right thing, but it did feel a bit disingenuous at the same time to turn up at the funeral of someone you really didn't care for.

I swept the thorns Imogen discarded from the roses and set about keeping the rest of the store floor clean and tidy. It was amazing how quickly the store became overrun with stray leaves and stalks and fallen petals. There was never a moment where I wasn't navigating different responsibilities at work. It helped that I naturally paid attention to the smaller details, and I enjoyed working with my hands—even if that did mean cleaning. You had to be comfortable wearing many hats in this game.

Imogen soon finished the big arrangement. Before she started the next one, she had a birthday bouquet. The flowers had been ordered by the birthday girl's husband, and he'd requested white roses and white camellias with our greenery of choice. I thought it was a splendid suggestion. The camellia symbolized love and affection, and I could feel the strength of this man's love for his wife even through a phone conversation.

I left Imogen in charge and went out to make deliveries. My Range Rover was packed, and I'd had to engage in a squawking fight with Norman, who wanted to accompany me. The last thing I needed was a temperamental parrot in tow, so I left him another bundle of banana chips. Normie sighed happily. At least that bird was easily appeased.

After dropping off the birthday white bouquets, I drove back past the church. It was a beautiful day, and I felt the urge to visit Jeremy's grave. Maybe it was the fuss the women in my life were making over this dinner with Alex. It had been forever since I'd had dinner with any man—even if it was merely to make up numbers. Of course, it wasn't like I was betraying Jeremy—I'd been on my own for a long time now, with not even a hint of a date. And I liked it that way. Just me, my coven, and our familiars.

Now, even if I hadn't accepted an actual date, the favor I was doing Alex had all the trappings of a date. I wanted to visit Jeremy and let him know.

I parked by the church and realized that a single white camellia had come loose. I took it as a sign. I took the single flower, enjoying the idea of sharing a bloom from the store we'd set up together.

Unlike Char, who had confessed her fear of graveyards, I felt peaceful walking through the church's cemetery. I was accustomed to my mom's relationships with the departed, so I didn't share the same fear of ghosts. In fact, I was comforted to sense that spirits were around me. But any sense of peace was shattered as I recalled Elizabeth's terrible scream at choir practice and Dolores's red-faced shame at being accused of spoiling the altar cloth. I did my best to shake off the feeling, but something was sticking to me.

I soon found the spot where Jeremy was buried and laid the camellia on the pale-gray stone. The inscription read: *Always in our hearts.* I plucked a few weeds, which had sprung up in the warm weather from the surrounding grass.

"Miss you, always," I whispered to the grave. "I hope you know that." I told him about Alex and how I'd agreed to have dinner with him. While I was there, I also told him how well the shop was doing and, of course, I had to tell him about Mick and poor Dolores. Jeremy hadn't cared for Dolores ever since we'd first opened our florist shop and she'd complained there'd be too much traffic near her cottage. Still, he would be horrified that she'd been murdered. I chattered on as I tidied up his grave, and then I told him I was so busy at the shop that I'd better get going.

The birds struck up their song then, and I strained my neck upward, cupping a shading hand above my eyes as I scanned the sky to see where the beautiful sound came from. I could see nothing but flickering brightness, the sun's rays lapping against my eyelashes. In a way, it was better not being able to see the birds. Like this, I could imagine they were singing just for me. Their song seemed to arise from out of the deep blue. A sign from Jeremy, perhaps, that he heard me and was wishing me well.

But the gentle moment was broken by the sound of raised voices.

I stood, dusting down the soiled knees of my Levi's, and then cupped a hand over my eyes again to squint across the graveyard. It was the vicar and Elizabeth Sanderson. But whatever were they arguing about? I listened carefully and realized that it was just Elizabeth's voice that was raised. I couldn't hear the vicar at all.

As I went closer, it became abundantly clear that it was Elizabeth who was the irate one of the two. She was gesticulating wildly, flapping her arms around and repeatedly pointing at a tree. In contrast, the vicar stood still, firmly in control. I felt a swish of disturbance—an unsettling, prickling feeling. The peace and tranquility I felt at Jeremy's graveside were swiped away.

Following a hunch, I went closer to see if I could make out what was ailing Elizabeth so. She had been distraught outside Dolores's cottage when she realized her friend was dead, and although I'd been less than impressed with how she handled Dolores's attempt at an apology note, I recognized sorrow when I saw it. Whether that sorrow was propelled and intensified by guilt, well, of that, I couldn't be so certain.

I kept my distance, not wanting to interrupt something so personal, but I wasn't alone for long.

Bernard Drake, the organist (and former warden who'd

been bullied so badly by Dolores that he quit), joined me. I'd learned a little about auras from Jessie Rae, and I was able to pick up some of the stronger ones. Bernard Drake's aura was a true, light pink—a rarity. The color represented a gentle soul, and he radiated a pleasant, loving energy. I knew that the color also indicated that he was deeply sensitive and a romantic, with the ability to keep the romance alive and well in relationships. Oh, if only you could bottle Bernard's aura and sell it.

I felt immediately more comfortable with Bernard standing beside me, and for the first time, I wondered if he had a natural healing tendency. His smile was a reminder to be gentle with each other and all of earth's creatures. I think the fact that, despite the weather, he was wearing charming brown tweed trousers and a golfing top also enhanced his approachable nature. I'd never understand the British countryside dress code.

I asked him if he knew what was happening, and he told me that poor Elizabeth had gone to pieces over the murder. "She's been inconsolable. We've been too scared to leave her alone. Been taking it in shifts, so there's always someone with her. To think of such a terrible thing happening in our own village."

It was a phrase I'd heard a lot over the past couple of weeks. No one liked to think that their village could ever house disaster, but trouble would seek them out.

"I was there when Dolores was discovered," I said. "And Elizabeth was distressed then, but has she really not calmed down?"

Bernard shook his head sadly. "No. She's taking it very badly that they parted on such bad terms. And what's making it worse is the vicar's plan for her burial site. Dolores always wanted to be buried near the church, under a tree that blossoms every spring, but the vicar says there's no room there. Elizabeth wants to honor Dolores's dearest wish."

"Oh dear. Is there not another suitable plot?"

"No. In fact, he's burying her right at the back of the graveyard in an obscure spot where there's terrible trouble with a certain noxious weed."

"Ragwort?"

"Ah yes, exactly."

"I know it well. Ragwort looks cheery enough with its bright-yellow daisy-like flowers, but it's full of toxins. I have to get rid of it in my garden all the time. Got special clothes for it. I know it's fatal to horses and cattle, but if the sap is absorbed through human skin, it can damage the liver. Not an ideal spot for a grave."

"Elizabeth thinks it might deter visitors, though perhaps she is worrying a bit too much."

We watched the vicar and Elizabeth until it became clear that the vicar was successfully calming her down.

"We're so lucky to have William as our vicar here," Bernard said wistfully. "Believe me, we've not always had such an approachable leader. William is a good man. You know, it's said that there are three Gs that can corrupt a man of the cloth. Girls, Gold, and God."

"I've never heard that before," I admitted.

Bernard went on to explain that women or money have ruined many a good man, and that extended to clergymen as well. "The worst G of them all, in my opinion, is that some of them even come to believe they *are* God, not His servant." He shuddered. "Power can corrupt even the most open of hearts."

"Goodness," I murmured and felt a strange whisper of an emotion that I couldn't quite place.

We were silent for a moment and then I remembered Bernard's comment about the communion wine at the choir practice, which had ended abruptly after the altar cloth incident.

"Bernard, could you explain more about the communion wine at the church? You said it's always locked up in the vestry. Did you ever find out how it got into the chalice during the choir practice?"

"Ah yes," he said, scratching the gray stubble on his cheek. "Well, as you know, the communion wine is kept locked in the vestry, and it's the warden's job to bring out enough for a communion service. It's then blessed, poured into the chalice, and blessed by the vicar again before being taken out to the altar. It's a routine thousands of years old. But all that happens right before the service. There is no reason for the wine to be in the chalice during the afternoon on a weekday." He dropped his voice a notch, although we were alone. "I'm glad I'm the organist now, and not the warden, as Rebecca is terribly upset. Technically, she's the one in charge, and people are starting to ask her some uncomfortable questions."

"I can imagine," I said.

"Anyone could forget to take the wine back to the vestry, of course, but it caused so much damage and such a row that she's taken it very hard. Especially with the subsequent death of Dolores."

"It's just awful," I agreed. "You always think you'll have

time to mend a relationship. You never think, *this could be the last time I'll ever have a chance.*" I thought again of Jeremy. We hadn't argued on his last day, thank goodness, but we hadn't done anything especially loving, either. It was a normal day. I'd kissed him goodbye when he went off riding, reminded him to be home in time for dinner out as we'd been invited to dinner with friends. I don't even think I said, *I love you.* He knew it, of course, but still, I always wished I'd said it.

"Could I say something in confidence?" Bernard asked. "You might be the most discreet person in the village."

"Of course," I said, a little flattered.

"Personally, I suspect the wine spillage was a premeditated crime."

I didn't want to believe that of Dolores, but it did make sense. "That's what Elizabeth thought, too," I said.

"It doesn't look good for Dolores, rest her soul," Bernard replied sadly. "But no good can come from speaking ill of the dead. No doubt she's gazing down on us now, wishing us well."

It was a comforting thought from a comforting man. He said goodbye and made to head back to the church, but turned at the last minute. "Do you know what's the saddest thing of all? Rebecca managed to get the worst of the red wine out of the altar cloth. A few sprays of a specialist stain detergent and I bet it would have looked as good as new. Dolores would have been comforted had she known." He shook his head. "Now that the cloth has such bad associations, I doubt we'll ever use it."

CHAPTER 16

*I*mogen and I worked overtime to get the flowers done for Alex's special dinner. Imogen had done an amazing job with the larger bouquets while I'd stuck with the more casual arrangements. It had been a dream-come-true commission. Expense was no issue and showstopper was the name of the game. Our creations were magnificent, full of vivacity and flair—sure to bring life and color to the castle.

We loaded the van together, huffing and puffing beneath the weight of so many flowers, suffering somewhat under the warmth of the sun.

Imogen returned to the shop while I drove carefully to Fitzlupin Castle. I was excited to see what the staging company had managed, and nervous too that they couldn't have done much with such a short time frame. I really wanted Alex to bag this new client as we'd both put so much effort into it.

Now that I was getting to know Alex, that aloof but polite exterior of his was melting away to reveal someone warm and gracious—even a bit insecure at times. He was also surprisingly down to earth—not at all the grandiose titled wine importer people round here made him out to be. I wondered why he didn't let more people see that side of him.

I arrived at a scene of great activity at the castle. A moving van was parked out front, and a couple of beefy men were carefully unloading a large mirror while a team of gardeners were mowing the front lawn and generally tidying up. Before unloading my flowers, I imbued the blooms with good fellowship and goodwill.

I picked up one of the smaller arrangements intended for the dining room when a tall man with chiseled arms said, "Let me help you with those." I wasn't sure which outfit he belonged to, but I was only too happy to accept the help. He lifted my arrangements as if they weighed no more than the colored feather Norman had tried to foist upon me last night for a brooch. I got him to bring one of the bigger displays to the entrance hall and said I'd get the rest later. I needed to make sure the space was ready for flowers.

Inside, the castle seemed to be swarming with people, so unlike what I'd experienced the last time I was here. It took me a moment to adjust. I could not believe how different the castle looked already.

The floors were gleaming beneath rugs that looked as though they'd always been there. The beaten-up furniture was gone and in its place comfortable, modern sofas mixed with antique pieces that clearly belonged to the castle. The windows sparkled from a fresh cleaning, and the whole place smelled of beeswax and lemon. I wandered through the rooms, searching for Alex, but there was no sign of him, so I went to set up.

In the dining room, a stylish woman was directing two

much younger women who were hanging gorgeous brocade curtains. "More drape to the left," she commanded to the women perched on stepstools.

On the polished floor was a Persian rug I'd have loved in my own house. The sideboards gleamed and the dining table sported a white linen cloth and freshly polished silver and glassware. There were a lot of crystal glasses. No doubt we'd be treated to numerous interesting vintages from Alex's cellar this evening.

I went to the side table where the enormous crystal vase I'd picked out earlier, as well as five similar vases, were ready for me to fill. I placed the first of the semi-casual arrangements into the waiting vase and fiddled with blooms until I was happy. As I moved around, I caught the attention of the woman directing the curtain operation. She cast a critical eye over the flowers and then nodded her approval. A flush of relief rose in me, and suddenly I realized that I had been worried about doing a good job for Alex.

I smiled back at the woman. "I can't believe the transformation you've made in such a short time."

"It's a tight deadline, but I've had worse," the woman replied, as she came toward the side table. She inclined her head and sniffed deeply at my bouquet.

"Ruby Calcot," she said, extending a slender hand, her wrist encircled by a thick gold bracelet.

"Peony Bellefleur of Bewitching Blooms," I said, shaking hands.

Ruby appeared to be in her forties and had the polished air and accent of someone who'd grown up wealthy. She wore businesslike linen trousers and a loose linen jacket. Her makeup and jewelry were impeccable. It was clear she was the brains of the operation and left the heaving and sweating to underlings.

The two women climbed down from their stepladders, and we all stood back to admire the perfect drape of the curtains.

"Beautiful," Ruby said. "Now, one of you fetch the throw cushions for the drawing room, and where are we with lamps?"

The two women grabbed their stools and scampered off. With help from the burly-armed man, I brought in the rest of the flowers and, if I do say so myself, the transformation was amazing. Between the cleaning, the staging, and the flowers, the castle interior now appeared welcoming, bright, and cared for.

I was tweaking a big arrangement in the drawing room and Ruby was placing some of the Fitzlupin family treasures on freshly polished table surfaces when Alex walked in.

Ruby's face switched from business to pleasure in an instant. And I could see why. Alex looked great in dark jeans and a white and navy striped apron splattered with several stains. He was obviously cooking up a storm in the kitchen, but he looked more relaxed than I'd have imagined given his reclusive nature. He was clearly more comfortable with a busy household than I'd given him credit for.

"Ah, Peony," he said, grinning. "The flowers are looking incredible. What a transformation. I could smell the jasmine all the way in the kitchen."

Ruby cleared her throat.

"And the furnishings are, of course, exquisite. Fabulous, both of you."

Ruby flashed an impossibly-white smile and tucked a strand of hair behind her ear.

"Just popping into the garden for more chervil," he said. "Let me know if you need anything."

We both watched Alex leave, and I can admit that watching Alex walk away wasn't a hardship on the eyes.

Ruby turned to me and fanned her face. "I wouldn't mind being the lady to that lord. I'll tell you that for free."

I chuckled, wondering if she noticed how my gaze had also lingered.

"Do you know how a dish like Lord Fitzlupin has managed to stay single so long? Is he one of those confirmed bachelor types?"

I shook my head. "I don't know anything about Alex's personal life. He keeps himself to himself."

She glanced at her watch. It had a large, round face, no doubt important when time was of the essence. She nodded. "Good. On schedule. I only need to make sure the lavatory has the right towels and so on, and I think we're done here."

Ruby turned to me, and from her linen jacket, pulled out a business card. "If you ever need our services," she said with a charming smile. "Or perhaps we could collaborate in the future?" Her gaze went to my bouquet again. "I like your style."

I glowed at the praise—it was so nice to have positive feedback from a woman who clearly knew her stuff. I handed over one of Bewitching Blooms' cards (a pale-rose color with a sweet-pea logo) and went to put the finishing touches to my other blooms, safe in the knowledge that the castle looked better than I could have imagined three days ago.

The rest was up to Alex.

WITH ALL THE bouquets and plants perfectly positioned, I closed the front door with a deep sense of satisfaction. Alex was outside, helping an enormous van park. He waved me over.

"I wanted to thank you again for agreeing to be my dining companion. George will pick you up at six-thirty p.m. so that you're here ahead of when the guests arrive at seven. Is that okay? Maybe it's too early for you with work?" He suddenly looked worried.

"It's absolutely fine," I said, laughing a little. "Imogen can close up for me tonight. But I don't need a chauffeur. I can drive myself."

Alex smiled. "The least I can do is open some criminally expensive wine this evening without you having to worry about driving home."

"Well, in that case, it sounds like a plan." I stared at Alex, surprised to see a sheepish expression creep into his eyes.

"What is it?" I asked.

"I may have told Louis Gagneux that you're my partner."

Something flickered between us, and then he broke the spell, stepping back. "Right. I'll let you get on. See you later."

And what was that about?

CHAPTER 17

*T*returned to Bewitching Blooms and asked if Imogen would mind if I left work early to get ready for the evening. I'd neglected to tell her that I was playing the part of Alex's partner and would somehow have to transform myself into a Lady with a capital L, but Imogen was more than happy to step in. "Frankly, I'd work overtime to hear a crumb of gossip from inside the castle."

We both worked hard for the next two hours, and then I left Imogen to close up. Normie flew over to Roberto's to wait for Char's shift to finish, promising me that he'd stay quiet on a tree outside until she was done. Although I didn't quite believe he would stay true to his word, I didn't have a choice. No way was I going to deal with his sardonic running commentary as I got myself ready for the evening's dinner. I packed him off with more banana chips and hoped that would hold him until the end of Char's shift.

I drove home with an unfamiliar excitement bubbling in my stomach. It had been a long time since I'd put on a dress and done my hair. A long time since I'd had a gourmet meal or vintage wines. It had been a long time since I'd felt my heart fluttering. I'll tell you—it was not at all unpleasant.

At home, I found Owen in the garden, hammering and muttering, going at the stone path with the ferocity of a demon.

I called out a hello, and Owen glanced up in surprise. "Peony, I was hoping to get the path finished for you before you came home from work. You finish early on Fridays?" He wiped the muck from his hands on his green gardening trousers.

"Not usually." I laughed. "But today, yes." I decided against explaining why. I was touched that Owen was finishing the path and told him that he needn't have worried himself. "I could have managed the rest on my own."

"It was a good distraction," he admitted. "I still feel angry with myself for letting Mick out of my sight. I also feel angry *with* Mick. I guess I'm just angry. So, I'm taking it out on the stone, and later I'll go to the gym to lift weights."

I told him to stop for a bit and come inside for some tea. I needed Owen to know that none of this was down to him.

I stepped inside the kitchen and put the kettle on, calling him when the tea was ready. Owen washed his hands at the sink before sitting at the table.

Putting a plate of shortbread beside the tea things, I told him to help himself. "I think Mick was going to do whatever Mick felt like doing," I said, brushing a stray leaf from my jeans. "He's that kind."

"I recognize it," Owen said, "because it was a lot like how I used to be." He paused and took a cup of breakfast tea, pouring milk into it slowly, thoughtfully. "Which is also why

I'm having a hard time believing that Mick had it in him to kill an old lady."

I nodded. "So, you feel he's innocent, too."

"Innocent of murder. Yes. I've been inside," he said. "You get to know what people are in for and why. Mick's a fool, but I don't think he's a killer."

"I've been thinking the same. So has Char, as you know," I said. "But if that's the case, then who did kill Dolores?"

Owen stared into his cup of his tea as if the answer might be there, which—according to Jessie Rae, who was a dab hand at reading tea leaves—it might well be. Owen's face darkened, and I could tell something was tormenting him.

"Do you have an idea of who it might be?" I asked quietly.

Owen appeared upset. "It's Gillian," he said finally. "She was really complaining about how rude Dolores was to her in your shop."

"At Bewitching Blooms?" I said, puzzled. And then I remembered the awkward exchange they'd had at the beginning of this week.

Gillian had joined the WI, and Dolores hadn't even bothered saying hello before chastising Gillian for buying the church flowers rather than making the bouquet from her own garden. The younger woman had stiffened and, as soon as Dolores was out of earshot, complained about how gossipy and judgmental the older woman was. I recalled how desperately Gillian wanted to belong in Willow Waters now that her husband had passed away. But enough to kill?

However, even Norman had recalled heated words between the two women. Was it possible?

"But why risk everything over being accepted by a small town?" I thought it was interesting that neither of us had trouble believing Gillian capable of murder. Unlike Mick, she seemed cool and calculating enough to remove someone who was getting in her way by whatever means that took.

Owen sipped his tea, and I thought he was taking a moment to gather his thoughts. "It's not merely about fitting in. If she felt like she had to leave Willow Waters, that would mean leaving Lemmington House behind. That woman adores her home. It's her castle. She's a determined woman, and I believe she's determined to make the people of Willow Waters accept her." Since he lived and worked on the Lemmington House property, I imagined he knew her pretty well.

When we'd finished our tea, Owen went back outside to finish the path, and I went upstairs to shower. I needed to wash away the day's grime and figure out how to get glamorous. It had been too long since I'd dressed up to the nines, and I was surprised by how much I was looking forward to it.

Although Char, Hilary, and my mom had all put forward more suggestions and made countless offers of loaning clothes, I decided in the end to stick to my plan of coming as myself—well, the best bits of me.

In the back of the wardrobe, tucked away in a dry-cleaning bag, was a vintage YSL dress which I'd picked up many moons ago in a thrift store in California when Jeremy and I were on vacation. It had been a lavish purchase, bought to wear to one of Jeremy's colleague's wedding receptions and then (criminally) never worn again. We'd been so busy setting up the store that any notion of fancy dos had been pushed out of my mind.

Upstairs, I unzipped the dress from its protective jacket and hoped the dress still fit. It was jet black, high-necked but sleeveless, with ruched darting that cinched the waist. The hem fell to just over my knees and the silk swished when I walked. I stared at the dress for another few minutes, wondering if it was too much. After all the fuss and care Alex had gone to to get the castle ready, I felt it was my duty to *bring it.* Especially if I was going to be masquerading as his partner. And Madame Gagneux would surely look chic—she was French, after all. I shrugged. If not now, when?

Blue seemed to agree because out of nowhere she lumbered up the stairs and into the bedroom, settling on my bed with a contented purr.

"That settles it," I said to Blue, bending to stroke her orange fur, pausing at her cheeks where she most liked to be tickled.

I hung the dress on the side of the wardrobe door and went to run myself a steaming hot shower.

The water rinsed away the day, and I used a geranium and orange aromatherapy gel to reinvigorate and then a matching oil to soften my skin—the excess of which I massaged into the ends of my hair.

I had thought about asking for Hilary's help to create some kind of sleek chignon, but contemplating my long, wet hair in the mirror, I was suddenly determined again to look as natural as possible.

I took a seat at my dressing table and sectioned my hair and then wrapped the strands around a barrel brush and carefully blow-dried each section until I'd created a gentle wave running through the lengths. I'd forgotten the simple pleasure of preparing for an evening out.

I even took time to make up my face with more than my

usual swipe of mascara and lipstick. When I'd finished, I regarded myself. "Not too shabby," I said to the mirror.

Blue meowed back from her position at the end of the bed. I took it as an agreement.

I was zipping up the silk dress when there was a knock at the door. I heard whispered giggling. Groaning, I said, "Come in."

Char, Hilary, and Jessie Rae piled into my bedroom like one six-legged snickering teenager. But their laughter stopped when their gazes locked on me.

"What is it?" I asked, suddenly nervous. "Too much?"

"Oh no, lassie, it's not too much," my mom said. "You look beautiful."

"She's right," Hilary said, "I don't think I've ever seen you all dressed up like that. It suits you."

Even Char, whose go-to response for anything was sarcasm, let out a wolf whistle and said, "Smokin' hot."

I blushed.

Norman flew in and said, "Didn't know you had it in you, Cookie."

"I'm not sure how long I can stand in these heels," I complained, scowling down at the vintage Louboutins my mom had discovered and bought me for my birthday. I could see she was pleased to see me wearing them.

"But what about my feather?" Normie cried out. "It's very special."

Char's head had disappeared inside my wardrobe and when she re-emerged, she was brandishing my burgundy pashmina. "You'll need this later," she said in a mom-voice I'd never heard from her before. "And you can fasten it with my brooch." She slipped a slim silver brooch from the back pocket of her jeans. "It's one of the few things I took with me from home," she said quietly. And then she wrapped the pashmina around my shoulders and fastened it with the brooch.

Hilary picked up my black clutch from the dressing table, popped my lipstick, keys, and phone inside—and then took Norman's feather from Char and slipped it through the loop of the handle. It looked perfect, and the rest of Norman's feathers seemed to plump up with pride.

"I think that's you done, lassie," Jessie Rae said. "My beautiful daughter," she said, coming to kiss me on the cheek.

The doorbell rang, and Normie flew to the window. "Your chauffeur awaits," he said gallantly in a pitch-perfect posh English accent.

CHAPTER 18

*G*eorge opened the doors to Alex's dark-green Jaguar.
He was wearing a very swanky charcoal suit.
Frankly, it was a relief George was outfitted so
smart as I was beginning to think I'd overdone it with the
cocktail dress and heels. Maybe you were thinking the same,
but I was doubly reassured as George bowed his head a frac-
tion and said, "Good evening, miss. You look as lovely as a
painting."

"I hope not one of those medieval oil paintings of washer-
women," I replied, laughing.

"Of course not," George said, clearly horrified.

I quickly realized tonight was going to be one of those
evenings where I'd have to keep my off-beat humor on the
down-low.

"Just joking, George," I said, settling into the leather of the
back seats at his insistence. "And you're looking exceedingly
dapper yourself."

As he started the engine, George checked his rear-view
mirror, and I caught the twinkle in his eyes. "It's like the old

days, miss," he said, and I could tell that he missed them. "You're in for a pleasant surprise when you see the house."

I smiled as I gazed out of the window, excitement and nerves mounting in equal measure.

We soon pulled into the long driveway, and I marveled at how welcoming the castle now appeared. It was glowing with warm lights which shone through the windows and the entrance.

When George opened the front door for me, I got my first glimpse of the whole place finished. The hallway looked incredible. The chandelier that hung from the high ceiling gleamed from a recent wash. An enormous Persian rug covered the worn floors. There were table lights, floor lamps, and, of course, my bouquets. I inhaled the luxurious scent of all those white, waxy flowers, pleased with the glorious first impression they gave.

George took my pashmina, hung it in the cloakroom, and told me that Alex was in the kitchen. "He's barely left the stove all day," he whispered.

"Perfectionist?" I asked.

"Oh, Ms. Bellefleur, you've no idea."

"Call me Peony, please. I hope Alex isn't planning to spend all night in the kitchen." I didn't want to be stuck entertaining a French vintner and his wife all by myself. What I knew about wine would fit in a sherry glass. With plenty of room left over.

George explained that his great-niece, June, was going to be serving this evening with his wife supervising the proceedings. "Alex has orders to stay out of the kitchen."

"Good."

The kitchen was a hub of warmth, jazz playing over the

speakers. A young woman was polishing the silverware, and the woman I assumed to be George's wife was standing next to Alex at the counter. They turned my way as George announced my arrival.

"Peony has arrived," he said grandly, as if I hadn't been in this very kitchen just a few hours ago.

Alex's face softened, and he said, "Wow, you look spectacular, Peony."

I couldn't help but feel flattered. "And you don't look so bad yourself," I replied. "Minus the apron, of course."

Alex was wearing a dark-gray, definitely designer suit. No doubt the apron would be swapped for a jacket, and hopefully soon. He looked, frankly, adorable—between the high-end suit, the apron, and, well, him.

Alex explained he was putting the finishing touches on the appetizer. "It's Raki-battered purple broccoli with a sivri biber sauce," he said proudly.

The kitchen smelled delicious but also looked organized. I had a feeling that the evening was off to an excellent start.

"Peony, this is Annabel, who's kind enough to let me play in the kitchen."

"Oh, get away with you. He's as fine a chef as any you'll find in London," she assured me. Annabel was a solid-looking woman in her late fifties with a frizz of white hair and rosy cheeks. She wore a serviceable apron and seemed well able to take over from Alex.

I only realized George had left the room when he returned with Alex's jacket.

"Come now, sir," he said, gently, gesturing for Alex to remove his apron. I noticed that his white shirt wasn't yet buttoned to the neck and a small curl of black chest hair peeked through.

Annabel jerked her chin at me, and I realized it was my job to take the chef out of the kitchen and turn him into the evening's host.

"Can you show me round before the guests arrive?" I asked Alex. "I'd love to see what Ruby did after I left."

Alex glanced from Annabel to me to George and accepted that he was outnumbered. "Okay, okay, I'm going. Keep an eye on that sauce, will you? It's—"

"All under control," Annabel said good-naturedly.

Alex and I left the kitchen. Maybe you won't believe this, but I could have sworn he stole sidelong glances at me. Maybe I needed to crack out the YSL dress more often.

He led me into the drawing room, and it really did look perfect. It was still a castle, but also a comfortable home.

"Ruby and her team are fantastic," I said.

"Absolutely. She works her staff hard, though. I'd be terrified if she was my boss."

I laughed. "I'm positive that Ruby would be less tough on you than others."

Alex's eyes widened with surprise, and I wondered if I'd said too much.

"I'm sure Monsieur and Madame Gagneux will love Willow Waters," I said, to change the subject. "At least you didn't have to put them up." I couldn't imagine Ruby and her staging crew could have managed bedrooms as well in the short time frame they'd had.

"No. They're staying at The Tudor Rose. I'm sure they'll be more comfortable there."

"I hope they don't hear about the murder," I said, thinking

that if they wandered into Roberto's, they'd hear about nothing else.

"I've been so busy I nearly forgot. Have there been any developments?"

"Not that I've heard." I hesitated, then said, "I saw Owen this afternoon. Neither he, nor Char, believe that Mick killed Dolores."

Alex raised his eyebrows. "Didn't stop him running, though, did it?"

"He told us he was lying low in Willow Waters because he was wanted for theft and fraud. He admits to being a thief but emphatically denies he murdered Dolores."

Alex didn't appear convinced. "As he keeps saying."

"It does make sense though, as to why he'd run. He got in with a bad crowd. He's already been in prison once. If he was convicted of murder, he'd go back and not come out for a very long time, if ever."

"That's tough. But I'm not so sure Mick's innocent."

"According to Char, Mick tried to get away from the people he was mixed up with, but no one would hire him, and he got pulled back into crime. He swears he wants to do better."

Alex's expression turned thoughtful. "Sounds a bit like what would have happened to Owen if Alistair hadn't been so openhearted with his job offer."

I nodded. "That's what Owen says. Oh, he's furious with Mick as he tried to help him and look what happened? But he doesn't think Mick is a killer." I paused and stared Alex straight in the eyes. "He'd have got away, too, if he wasn't attacked by a wolf."

He smiled. "I believe I told you we haven't had wolves in

the UK in hundreds of years. It must have been a dog. A big one." Alex stopped in front of a bookcase. "Look, Ruby even got her team to dust the books. I never would have thought of that. She also pulled out the best art ones to display on the coffee table."

Alex was clearly being evasive.

It was hard to be frustrated when he looked so handsome, but I was determined not to be swayed from my tack. "Still kind of funny that a dog would attack a man for no reason and then run away."

"No doubt it thought the running human was a danger."

"You seem to understand the way dogs think." Our conversation had taken on a ping-pong-like back and forth, but now there was an awkward moment.

Alex opened his mouth to say something, but the bell rang.

We heard George open the front door, and Alex said, "That's our cue. Are you ready? Goodness, I almost forgot to tell you our origin story. We met in Café Roberto a year ago, locked eyes over a macchiato, and have been together ever since."

"Must have been a good macchiato," I said.

Alex took my arm and escorted me from the library to the hallway where George was greeting Madame and Monsieur Gagneux. I was not surprised to find a very chic couple before me.

Based on his round belly, Monsieur Gagneux clearly enjoyed his food and wine. He had white hair and impish blue eyes, though he was dressed with fashionable elegance. Madame Gagneux was a magnificent sight, and I was glad to have pulled out the stops. Tall, with impeccable posture, she was wearing a beaded emerald-green dress. She was very slim compared to her husband and had that effortless elegance so common in French women.

After greeting both guests with a hearty handshake and two kisses for Madame Gagneux, Alex made a formal introduction.

"Louis and Violetta, may I introduce you to Peony Bellefleur."

Louis kissed me grandly on both cheeks and said how happy he was to meet me.

Violetta followed suit. She smelled like freesia. "*Enchanté*," she said.

I'd imagined they might be difficult guests, as Louis Gagneux had been so specific about his requirements before doing business with someone, but both husband and wife exuded a warmth that immediately put me at ease. They complimented Alex multiple times on his wonderful home, and I felt the shift in Alex's demeanor as he relaxed, safe in the knowledge that all the hard work had been worthwhile.

Louis produced a bottle of champagne as though pulling a rabbit from a hat. When Alex would have reached for it, he tutted and pulled the bottle back. "But, no. I have brought you something special from my cellar, but I have told my wife so much of your famous nose. You must show her, *mon ami*."

Alex appeared somewhat surprised, but he was used to being teased about his incredible sense of smell. "Very well. Do you plan to blindfold me?"

"That will not be necessary. I will open and pour the wine, and you will impress the ladies."

I hoped Alex passed the test. We'd worked so hard to make everything perfect. What if his famous nose didn't extend to champagne? Would Louis take his business elsewhere?

To my amazement, Alex rose and pushed a button near the grand fireplace. George materialized instantly.

"Ah, George, could you bring four champagne flutes, please?"

As though they were always ready and waiting. George disappeared and returned in moments with a silver tray (gleaming from a recent polish) and four delicate champagne flutes, also gleaming.

Alex was made to sit on the sofa that looked as though it had graced this grand room for years instead of a matter of hours. We settled ourselves, and then I heard the distinctive pop of a champagne cork. Louis Gagneux came forward with four glasses of palest gold bubbling wine. His eyes twinkled as he offered the tray first to me, then to his wife, and finally to Alex. He took his own, set down the tray, and sat beside his wife and opposite Alex and me.

We all waited.

Alex shook his head as though to say, 'I'm not a performing monkey,' but then he closed his eyes and held the glass under his nose. "Apricot and orange. A hint of toast, and is that a note of jasmine?" He took a sip and smiled with pleasure. "Bollinger, of course."

"*Très bien, mon ami.* But which year?"

I could not believe Louis was making Alex guess the year.

The vintner turned to me and said, "He has many to choose from, as the house was founded in 1829."

Alex took his time sipping. "Pre-World War II, obviously," he said. "It's held up remarkably well. I taste a little wheat, the tiniest hint of mushroom, a trace of anise." Here he paused. "1936." He sipped again. "No. '37, I think."

Louis laughed and clapped his hands. "Did I not tell you, my dear?" he said to his wife, who appeared less enthusiastic, but still said Alex was very good.

I finally sampled my champagne. I'll be honest with you. I could have told you it was champagne and not prosecco. Probably. Other than that? I'd have been lost.

I'd seen Alex with coffee, but to pick a vintage of champagne? That was amazing.

Louis continued talking about Alex's famous nose. "He could be a top sommelier in Paris. He has the looks, the knowledge: everything." He turned to me. "My dear, wouldn't you like to live à Paris?"

I laughed. "I have to admit, I've never been."

Violetta gasped. "Peony, you must come visit us. At the chateau if you like, but perhaps it's better in Paris. We have a petite townhouse in the Marais. I'll take you shopping. And then to my favorite bistro." She flashed me a beautiful smile, her white teeth small and shining.

"Thank you." I sipped more champagne. It was hard to believe I was drinking something that had been made so long ago and had lasted so well. It was delicious as well as historical. I was going to have to watch myself this evening. Alcohol could loosen my control over my powers. I didn't want to be asked to pass the salt and send it floating across the table unaided.

I listened as the men caught up on mutual wine acquaintances. It was a fascinating insight into a world I really knew nothing about. But Violetta had stood and walked to the sideboard where one of my bouquets looked (if I said so myself) sensational.

"These are *très très chic*," she said.

Alex paused his conversation with Louis and told her that, in fact, I was a florist and all the flowers were of my design.

Louis looked delighted. "I smelled jasmine as soon as we entered. Flowers add to the ambiance of this magnificent home."

I smiled and thanked them for the compliment, content in knowing that my spell of welcome and enjoyment held within the delicate tips of the flowers was doing its magic.

We were getting on wonderfully when George came in to announce dinner. We moved into the dining room, and it really did look splendid.

I knew that Alex had chosen wines to complement his cooking and was excited to enjoy the evening ahead. We had a beautiful white wine with the first course of the freshest-tasting scallops done with a delicate green sauce. We took our time over our food, laughing and chatting.

When we got to the main course, which Alex had told me was a lamb dish, inspired by his time in Turkey, Alex brought out a wine in a decanter. "Now it is my turn to share a treasure from my own cellar with you."

Louis broke into a broad smile, and I caught sight of two pure gold teeth nestled in the right-hand side of his mouth. "Go on," he coaxed.

"Please, taste it."

The older man cocked a wry eyebrow. "I have not your nose, my friend, but I will indulge you."

As Alex had, he breathed and tasted, swirling the wine

around on his tongue. Finally, he opened his eyes. "You honor us. This is a fine Bordeaux. The deep plum, almost volcanic depth. More I cannot tell you."

Alex nodded. "Your nose is correct. It's a 1982 Château Grand-Puy from Lacoste in Pauillac. I'd say it's one of the best vintages of the century, especially for the wines of Bordeaux."

"A special wine indeed," Louis agreed, sipping again.

"That I'm honored to be sharing with such special guests," Alex replied.

The lamb was succulent and delicious and, even to my untutored palate, seemed to go brilliantly with the fancy wine.

"Your caterer is to be commended," Violetta said. "This is quite the special dish."

"Alex did the cooking," I replied before Alex could deflect the attention. "He is an excellent chef." I heard the pride in my voice and decided I definitely sounded like a contented girlfriend.

"Lucky girl," Violetta said. "Louis has never even peeled a carrot."

He shrugged his shoulders. "My talents do not lie in the kitchen." He seemed fine with that.

The conversation flowed, and the wine followed suit—everything sumptuous and decadent.

The rest of the evening flew by. And although I slowed down the consumption of wine, I ate and drank heartily, laughing and talking, and not once did it feel like I was putting on a show for Louis and Violetta. Not once did I remember that I was not, in fact, Alex's partner of one year. Too much Bordeaux, you're thinking? Well, maybe. But it was the nicest evening I'd had in a long time.

At the end of the night, long after the grandfather clock had chimed midnight, we walked Louis and Violetta to the door.

"My friend, you have been the most excellent host and chef. I will sign the contract in the morning, when I hope to tour your cellar. I find your home and your lovely partner simply delightful."

George was waiting with the Jaguar to return them to The Tudor Rose. Then he'd return for me. I kissed the couple on both sets of cheeks, feeling very continental indeed.

Alex shut the door and turned to me with an expression of happiness shot through with relief. "We did it," he said, and took both my hands. "I can't thank you enough, Peony. You have gone above and beyond. All the advice, the flowers, the wonderful, wonderful company." Alex's cheeks were flushed, and though he held his liquor like the pro that he was, I could tell he was a tad tipsy.

So was I. And the feeling was wonderful. I was suffused with a warmth that began in the tips of my toes and ended in my fingertips. But I was certain it wasn't just the wine. I had enjoyed every moment. From designing the flowers to sitting by Alex's side this evening.

I gazed into his startling gray-blue eyes and knew that my own sparkled with the same attraction.

"I'll get your pashmina," he said softly.

I watched as he walked through the chandelier-lit hallway and suddenly felt immeasurably sad that his home was so beautiful and warm because of a staging company, and soon they'd be back to take everything away again, returning the castle to its former emptiness.

Why didn't Alex furnish this place properly? It wasn't like

he was short of money. What was holding him back? I sensed a deep loneliness here. And then I thought of my own home, unconventional but full of family. Yes, that's exactly what my motley crew of women were: family. It felt good to be returning to Char and Hilary and Jessie Rae tonight—even if they weren't quite as handsome as Alex.

Alex returned and draped the pashmina 'round my shoulders. He bent closer to me then, and kissed both my cheeks, French style. He lingered for a moment and as my heart raced, I closed my eyes, certain he was really going to kiss me, but he pulled away as the sound of the Jag's engine rumbled in the drive.

We stared at each other for a moment. I was confused. Had Alex held back because George was outside, or because he'd thought twice about going further with me?

"Thank you again, Peony," he said, his voice steady again, and more formal. He opened the front door. "Make sure to lock all your windows and doors when you get in because if Char's right about Mick, then a murderer is still at large in Willow Waters."

"Right," I murmured. "Of course. Goodnight." *Way to end the evening, Alex, with notions of a murderer on the loose.*

As I was making my way down the steps, he called out my name.

I turned and found that he was holding a single camellia from the big bouquet in the front hall. He came toward me and offered me the single flower. Even though I was the one who put the flower in the bouquet, I was charmed.

CHAPTER 19

*O*f course, the floaty feeling didn't last long. The second my key turned in the lock of my front door, it opened. I know what you're thinking, but it wasn't magic. It was Hilary.

"How was your evening?"

I laughed, and then shushed myself, conscious of waking the others. I whispered that it had been great.

"No need to whisper," Hilary said. "We're all in the kitchen—Normie, too. No one wanted to go to bed without hearing about your night."

I was as giddy as a teenager, enchanted by the castle and the food and the wine and the company. But any notion of privacy soon disappeared as Hilary led me to the kitchen where Char and Jessie Rae were giggling, two very large glasses of red wine in their hands. Blue was curled up in my mom's lap and even she raised her head enquiringly.

"How did the castle look?"

"What did you eat?"

"What were the French couple like?"

"Did Alex look handsome?"

"Did you kiss him?"

The questions came so thick and fast I couldn't tell who was talking. I kicked off my heels, refused a glass of red—I'd had more than enough—and set about telling the girls (and Normie) how the evening went. I spoke quickly, enjoying their rapt expressions—but aware that I needed to open the store tomorrow, and it was way past my usual bedtime. I mean, seriously.

They listened, quieter than I think they'd ever collectively been, and I stopped at the moment before Alex had kissed my cheeks.

"Why are you holding a camellia?" Char asked.

I'd forgotten I was still holding the bloom and tried not to blush as I told them Alex had given it to me as I was leaving.

"What a cheapskate," Norman said. "Giving you one of your own flowers."

"I think it's romantic," Char snapped back.

"The camellia is a symbol of love and devotion," Hilary said.

"I'm sure Alex didn't know that," I said, but the other women all exchanged a knowing look. I flushed. Argh, it was like being back at school all over again.

Trying to deflect any more attention, I asked about everyone's evening. "I know you haven't sat here all night waiting for me to come home." At least I hoped not.

Char's face darkened. "I had a phone call from Mick. He's been formally charged with murder."

I watched with growing alarm as her fists clenched. Worried that her anger might rise up and come out of her fingertips as fire, I placed my hands over hers. We had to be careful around Hilary—as well as my tablecloth.

"He's convinced he'll spend the rest of his life in prison," Char continued. She stared down at my hands on hers. "But he didn't kill Dolores," Char insisted. "I know he didn't."

I nodded. "Owen agrees with you," I said quietly. "And I trust your intuition."

Char's expression softened, and I watched, sadness in my heart, as her frustration turned to despair. "He doesn't have the money for a good attorney." She turned to Hilary.

I could sense what was coming even as Hilary sipped her wine unaware.

"Could you represent him? We'll find a way to pay you back."

Hilary sighed and put down her glass. "You know I would help you, Char, but I was a family lawyer, not criminal. I might know someone from university who could help. I'll put in a call tomorrow, but I can't promise anything."

Then, to my astonishment, Char appealed to Jessie Rae. "Could you contact Dolores and ask her what happened that afternoon?"

Was this really the same Char who'd scoffed at my mom's occult shop? Laughed off the offer of a tarot reading? Turned up her nose at crystals?

"Och, lassie, it doesn't work that way," my mom said. "The spirits come to me, not the other way round. If Dolores wants to communicate something, she'll have to make her own path back to this world. But if the police have it wrong, then we must help this poor young man ourselves."

"How?" Char asked.

"Break him out of jail," Normie suggested.

I shook my head at him. "To prove he's innocent, we have to find the murderer ourselves."

Hilary suddenly sat up straight. "It's late, but we're all awake, right? Let's adjourn to my room. I've been working on a project for university and borrowed a huge presentation board on an easel from the department to sketch out my notes. We can pool our ideas and make sense of this thing. Murderers leave clues, and we all live and work in this community. Surely we've seen or heard something useful."

It was a good idea. "Four heads are better than one," I said.

Norman squawked.

"Sorry," I said. "I meant five heads are better than one. Especially the colorful ones."

I ran upstairs to change into something more comfortable than a YSL cocktail dress. I was still holding the camellia, so I found a bud vase, filled it with water, and placed the bloom on the windowsill. I slipped into some old sweatpants and a T-shirt and made my way to Hilary's room at the other end of the landing.

Hilary's room was decorated more traditionally than the others. I'd wallpapered it in deep-mustard fleur-de-lis printed on thick textured cream paper. The curtains were also mustard velvet, pulled closed now, and the bed had a heavy mahogany frame and was an impressive presence in the center of the room. But Hilary had really made the space her own. One corner was converted into a home office and a floor lamp lit the space where a large desk, presentation easel, and enormous bookcase left you in no doubt as to how seriously Hilary took her studies. In fact, there were also books scattered across the floor and piled high on the bedside table.

However, don't think that the room wasn't also warm and cozy. Academic or not, this was a farmhouse, and you couldn't study the charm out of my home. I took a divan and stretched out, feeling my body relax and my mind switch on.

Char and Jessie Rae were already ensconced on two red poufs, and Hilary was standing by the easel, which held a huge pad of foolscap paper. Norman looked on from the top of the bookcase.

I caught a glimpse of Hilary's timeline of the Roman Triumvirate before she tore off the page and rummaged in her desk drawer, eventually pulling out a set of colored markers.

On the fresh page, she wrote *Dolores Prescott* and the date of her murder and the assumed time of her murder, which was shortly before Alex and I stumbled across Mick running from her house.

Beneath that, she wrote *SUSPECTS* and underlined it once with a bold flourish. Mick's name quickly followed.

"But he didn't do it," Char insisted. "That's the whole point of this exercise, to prove he didn't do it, not help the police by making him appear more guilty."

"That may well be the case, but we must disprove all the evidence the police have against him," Hilary replied.

I had never seen Hilary in lawyer mode before, and I was seriously impressed.

"There is no evidence," Char maintained.

"It's circumstantial, to be fair, though rather damning all the same." To Mick's name, she added that he was discovered at the scene, the body still warm, previously convicted, and on the run from the law.

I swallowed as I surveyed the board. It really didn't look

good for Mick. I could see why the police were adamant that they'd found their man.

"Now let's talk about other suspects," Char insisted. "I hear everything at Roberto's. What about Gillian Fairfax? The old bat—I mean the victim—Dolores said all kinds of nasty things behind her back. Gillian knew it, too, and I'd seen the way she glared at Dolores. It was chilling. If her eyes were weapons, Dolores would've been dead long ago."

"Gillian was pretty damning of Dolores at Bewitching Blooms earlier this week," I added. "Though really it was nothing compared to the distasteful way Dolores spoke to her about joining the WI. Honestly, I felt sorry for Gillian. Everyone loves jumping to conclusions about her."

"You get back what you put out," Jessie Rae said, her eyes closed in concentration.

Hilary wrote down *Gillian Fairfax* and the grudges she had against Dolores.

Jessie Rae opened her eyes. They were flashing with excitement. "Shouldn't we be finding out where Gillian was the day Dolores was murdered? We know she had motive, but did she have opportunity?"

It was great—but also unusual—to see Jessie Rae acting practical.

"Good point, Mom. She was in my store in the morning before the murder, buying flowers for the church. And she had that run-in with Dolores right in front of me. The day of the murder, I don't know."

"Char, why don't you ask Owen if he saw Gillian leave Lemmington House in the afternoon?" Hilary suggested. "Really, anything about her movements that day would be useful. We're calling the time of death five o'clock because that's when Mick came running out of the house. However, if he's telling the truth, she could have been killed some time before that."

"Alex said she was still warm," I reminded Hilary.

She nodded and said that given the warm weather, the body temperature would remain warm for longer than in the winter, which made sense.

"Ah," I said, "Gillian will be in tomorrow to collect her flowers for Sunday. I'll have a chance to have a casual chat with her, and see if I can find out anything useful."

"Good thinking," Hilary said.

Jessie Rae suggested Elizabeth Sanderson should be added to the list of suspects. "She had a motive in that she believed Dolores deliberately sabotaged her beautiful altar cloth. She was in my shop the day after it happened. I've rarely seen so much anger swirling around a person. It was a red and black cloud. You remember, Peony," she said, turning to me. "She stomped on your flowers."

"And tore up Dolores's apology card," I added. "Not that it was much of an apology. Even when saying she was sorry, Dolores was trying to blame the new warden." I recalled the terrible scene at the church with the altar cloth and the wine. "I did overhear Elizabeth saying she could kill Dolores for what she'd done. And Mom's right, she was behaving horribly in the store. But Elizabeth was devastated when she heard about her friend's murder. Inconsolable."

"Could have been a guilty conscience?" Jessie Rae suggested.

"A good way to appear innocent," Char said darkly.

"It's often the person closest to the victim who's the perpetrator," Hilary added. She added Elizabeth Sanderson's name to the board and listed the details we'd supplied.

"And where was Elizabeth Sanderson during the afternoon when Dolores was murdered?"

"She was in Roberto's," Char said. "I remember because she got pretty loud at one point. She was definitely still steaming mad at Dolores."

"Could she have murdered her old friend and then gone to the coffee shop?" That would be a great way to appear innocent, but could anyone really do that?

We fell silent, each of us thinking hard. Who else? Dolores upset everyone all the time with her snarky comments. But was it enough to commit such a dreadful crime?

"The organist at the church," I said suddenly. "He told me that there shouldn't have been communion wine in the chalice. Bernard Drake, his name is. He thinks the wine was put there on purpose. Dolores could have planned to ruin the cloth and make it look like an accident. She used to be the warden. She could easily get the key to the vestry—or slip in when no one was watching."

"Hmm," Hilary said thoughtfully. "Surely, anyone at the church that day had the same opportunity. Is there another, less obvious, suspect?"

I thought hard. What about the organist himself? Imogen had told me that Bernard Drake had to have therapy after Dolores bullied him when he was the warden.

He seemed like a genuinely nice man, but I was beginning to realize that genuinely nice people could do unspeakable things if pushed hard enough. I suggested we add him to the list. The most difficult task was going to be figuring out where everyone had been during the afternoon Dolores died.

"And what about the new warden?" Hilary asked. "Rebecca Miller? If she looked bad because Dolores Prescott deliberately put wine in the chalice when it shouldn't have been there, might that have pushed her over the edge, so to speak?"

"Add her name to the list," I said. I liked Rebecca, but you never knew what kind of resentment was lurking beneath the surface of a person. Maybe she'd been trying to find a way to get back at Dolores for making her look bad. Or maybe Dolores had driven her crazy too, complaining she wasn't doing the job right.

Char yawned, then, making the rest of us yawn, too.

"It's late," I said, "and I have to be up to open the store soon. Let's call it a night and see what we can learn about our suspects in the morning."

Hilary was going to find out what she could about Bernard Drake's and Rebecca Miller's movements on the day of the murder. I'd try to get more information from Gillian, and Char would ask Owen what he remembered of Gillian's movements that day. It didn't help that he'd been supervising Mick at my farmhouse, but hopefully he knew something useful. We weren't so much grasping at straws as out hunting for straws to grasp.

CHAPTER 20

*R*emembering Alex's parting words, I went to make a quick check on all the doors and windows downstairs before heading to my own bed.

The farmhouse often creaked and groaned—one of the charms of living in a Grade II listed building, so I was used to things going 'bump in the night' as it were, but as I made the rounds, something felt off. I couldn't pinpoint the feeling. It wasn't a threat. But I sensed a presence.

Following my instinct, I went to the kitchen to double-check the back doors. Everything looked normal. The cupboards were closed. The wine glasses were still on the table, their bellies still red with the last dregs of wine. The feeling was even stronger as I stood by the glass and looked out into the garden.

I held my breath. Who was out there?

I squinted closer to the glass, peering into the backyard. The plants and flowers were glowing in the light of the moon. Nothing seemed amiss. And yet? Why couldn't I shake this feeling?

I pressed my face against the glass and scanned the entire garden. And then I saw it. There was a wolf in the garden. A wolf, not a dog. It had the same long, proud body and elegant face as the one I'd seen the other week. The same hindquarters as the one I'd seen disappear into the forest earlier. No doubt about it. I was stunned to see it so close to my home. But I didn't feel afraid. On the contrary, I had the sense that the wolf was guarding the house.

It moved then and began to circle the perimeter. Striding in long-gaited loops. It was behaving like a guard dog. I smiled. And then, taking a risk, I unlocked and then opened the back door.

The garden was magical in the light of the half moon and the stars, glittering and twinkling in a clear sky.

The wolf was at the side of the house now, just out of sight. I wondered how he got into my garden, as surely he didn't take the road?

Following my instinct, I decided to leave the garden by the back. With delight, I noticed that Owen and Mick's path was now finished. Owen must have laid the final stone after I'd gone up to change earlier. I stepped lightly over the glittering stones until I reached the footpath, which led to a wooded area behind the farmhouse.

I imagine you're thinking I'm crazy—I mean, this was the exact opposite of what Alex had asked me to do to keep safe. But not for one second did I feel vulnerable. On the contrary, I felt more watched over and protected than ever.

I'd only followed the path for a trifle when I glimpsed a flash of something white on the ground. I went closer and saw it was a man's shirt. I turned in a circle, scanning the darkness around me. There was no one. Nothing. I picked up the shirt. I might not have Alex's nose, but right away, I knew the fabric held his fresh, woodsy scent.

I continued walking and soon found a pair of jeans and some heavy, well-worn boots. I knew without a doubt that they all belonged to Alex, and everything which had been percolating in my mind over the last few weeks came together and made sense. I folded the discarded clothes neatly, put his boots side by side beside a flat rock, and sat down to wait.

Then I checked myself. Wasn't a murderer on the loose? And here I was, a lone woman—no, a lone sitting duck—loitering in the deepest dark next to a creepy woodland? Despite the calm I felt, maybe I wasn't so clever.

So, by the light of the moon, I gathered a handful of small stones and made a circle on the ground. I said a quick protection spell.

"Earth, wind, fire, and water,
Hear these words from your daughter:
Let my mind be alert
Let my heart be true
Within this circle, safety surrounds me
Let this path be trouble free
Let no evil come to me.
As I will, so mote it be."

Time passed in a haze. My thoughts swirled, though not unpleasantly. I went over the evidence against each of our suspects. I thought of the scent of Alex's skin, the way his lips brushed my cheeks, and then I let the hypothesis I had about Alex swell and grow.

It was nearly dawn when I sensed someone approaching. The light was pearly gray, the air cool, birds singing their morning song. I couldn't see anyone, but I knew he was there.

"You can come out," I called out in a voice which sounded more confident than I felt.

To my relief, I heard Alex's deep baritone say, "Actually, I can't. Unless you'd like to leave my clothes where they are and turn your back."

I almost laughed. Even though I'd been certain I knew him, I hadn't had proof until now. Right. I had his clothes all folded up, and he was naked. "Sure," I said, and turned my back.

As I waited, I heard him behind me, pulling on his clothes.

After a moment, there was silence and I turned to find him fully dressed and obviously at a loss as to what to say. Well, I knew a thing or two about secrets and alternative lifestyles. It was no biggie. "So, you're a wolf when you're not a man," I finally said.

Alex cleared his throat. "Yes." I could see that he had no idea what I was going to do with this news. "No one's ever guessed my secret before. I don't know what to say. I-I hope this won't ruin our friendship."

"I've suspected for a while," I said gently, and laid a hand on his arm. I could feel his muscles through his shirt. "I'm not shocked," I said. "Please don't think that. I know how isolating it is to be different. You've been protecting yourself. I understand more than you could know."

I'd obviously said the right thing because Alex nodded and then took a seat on the rock. I followed suit.

"You've known that Baron Fitzlupin, the owner of the

local castle, is a werewolf?" he asked. Even he sounded surprised that the local lord was a shifter.

"Suspected. Now I know for sure. Thanks for keeping an eye on us, by the way."

"Very difficult to guard you when you won't stay inside the house. Be glad I wasn't the murderer."

Okay, the shock of being discovered was obviously wearing off.

"Well, you're here now," I said, not wanting to get into a stupid argument about overprotective men and how I could take care of myself.

"Can I trust you, Peony?" he asked. "With my secret, I mean."

I assured him that he could.

"It's an enormous relief, actually. Only George knows the truth. He helps me, you see, when I have no control during the full moon. He has to lock me in the old dungeon for the night. It's humiliating, but I don't like to be out then because my behavior can be unpredictable. The scratches on the floors at home are evidence of that. Other times, I can shift forms at will, like tonight, when I find it useful to use my animal senses and greater speed."

"So you could play guard dog," I said.

"Yes." His gaze dropped. "I admit I was patrolling the farmhouse to make sure you were all safe. I was worried."

"I appreciate it," I said, "but I promise you that we're not as helpless as we look." I paused then, toying with whether to divulge my own secret. I've always felt it's better to hold on to my secret until I'm absolutely certain about sharing it. I sighed and then put the urge to confess away again. "And I promise that your secret is safe with me. Always."

Alex's expression turned grateful, and then he tilted his head to the sky. "Dawn is coming. I should get home."

I nodded and as we stood, Alex gazed at me intensely. "I wish things could be different," he said. And then he was gone.

CHAPTER 21

I only managed a couple of hours of turbulent sleep before I had to get up and open the flower shop. I groaned at the alarm, and poor Blue meowed at me angrily as I disturbed her favorite sleeping spot on the corner of the bed. If only I'd had the foresight to ask Imogen to open for me today.

I practically threw myself into the shower, pulled on an old pair of comfy Levi's and smartened the look with my favorite pistachio-green linen shirt and gold hoop earrings. And lipstick. Man, how many times had a swipe of pink gloss saved me from looking sallow?

During my all-too-short night's sleep, I'd dreamed I could hear a wolf howling, flashes of dark fur, glittering gray-blue eyes. Although I'd had my suspicions about Alex's shifting nature, it had still been a surprise to see it in the flesh. Not that I did manage to catch a glimpse of his flesh. I mean, I had to let the poor man keep a semblance of modesty after he exposed his biggest secret.

After a quick breakfast of strong coffee and hearty

granola, I drove to the store on autopilot, sneaking out before Norman saw me. Don't think I'm mean—I just didn't have the energy for his wisecracks. Char would have to deal with her familiar today.

I went through the motions of a normal weekend morning, smiling, greeting, creating beautiful bouquets, ringing up orders, and taking payments. Imogen (blessedly) had been out on a date herself last night and was quiet, too. And so, although the bags under both our eyes were almighty, we got the job done, and I allowed myself a mental replay of yesterday's events, which I'd been denied by the girls at home.

The scent of Alex's skin had stayed with me, and I had to keep glancing up from my workbench to check he wasn't in the store.

At midday, Gillian arrived, and I felt a flurry of energy race through me. I was determined to find out everything I could to help find Dolores's real killer. Even if that meant asking uncomfortable questions. In my line of work, I found that you could get away with saying most things as long as you did it with a broad smile and a pleasant tone.

"Hi," I said, as Gillian swept into the store.

As usual, she was dressed impeccably: navy silk shirt and wide cream trousers and carrying a classic black Chanel purse.

"Hello, Peony," she said pleasantly. She was calm and assured, her honeyed voice soft. "I'm here to pick up the church flowers."

I nodded. "Of course." I retrieved the two arrangements I'd made, adding extra flowers and heft. "I think they turned out really well."

Gillian clapped her hands. "How wonderful! Aren't you an angel!"

Not quite, but it was the look I was going for. "Tell you what," I said. "I need some fresh air. How about I walk over to the church with you and carry one? Imogen will cover for me."

Gillian appeared delighted and accepted my offer gratefully. She even had the grace to compliment my bouquets. They were—if I say so myself—exquisite. Tulips, lots of daisies, peonies, a few roses and ferns for greenery. They could easily have come from her garden, if she could have been bothered to pick the blooms herself.

As we walked to the church, I initiated the usual pleasantries—a dollop of village news, followed by an inquiry into her tennis lessons. Gillian was well-schooled in small talk, and she chattered good-naturedly. As we passed Dolores's cottage, I saw her expression darken. Obviously, I jumped on it.

"Terrible business," I said, shaking my head. "A knife in the back. So awful."

"Awful," Gillian echoed. "I wouldn't wish such a vicious ending on my worst enemy."

I made some agreeing clucking sounds and silently bargained with Dolores's spirit to forgive me for what I was going to say next. "Sadly, she wasn't short of those."

Gillian turned to gaze at me over the bouquet. "Of what?" she asked pleasantly.

"Enemies," I replied. "Dolores had a real knack for rubbing people the wrong way."

Gillian wrinkled her elegant nose. "That may be so, but surely nowhere near enough to warrant a murder. Besides, they've arrested the culprit. Everybody is talking about it. An opportunist if ever I've heard of one. You know he was staying at poor Owen Jones's cottage, on my property. I'm not very pleased about it, I can tell you. I've been magnanimous in allowing Jones to stay on, even with his criminal past, but I won't have him bringing his jailbird friends to stay. Especially not when they murder people in my village."

Okay, so not what I'd been hoping for. Trust Gillian to make another woman's murder all about her. She sounded as convinced as everyone else in the village that Mick was the murderer. Could it be a perfect cover-up for her own sinister intentions? To be honest with you, I wasn't convinced that Gillian had it in her. Watching the way she handled the flowers—holding the bouquet away from her body as if the pollen might spill and stain her shirt—was enough to show me that she wouldn't have it in her to stab someone in the back.

She *did* have money, though. Oodles of it. Was it possible she paid someone else to do the terrible deed? Mick, for instance?

I no sooner had the thought than I dismissed it. Owen wouldn't have let Mick and Gillian be alone for a second.

We arrived at the church and entered its cool, dim interior. Gillian called out hello and then the vicar emerged from a side room. He appeared especially pleased to see us—I'm not sure if it was the abundance of flowers that brought such a warm welcome, or Gillian's bright smile. I was tempted to think the latter. Gillian was an especially attractive woman, and I'd seen the way men responded to her. He came toward the widow and stretched out his hands. She put her bouquet down on a pew, and he grasped both of her hands empathetically.

"How *are* you?" he asked in a gentle tone. It had been he who'd buried her husband a short while ago.

Gillian murmured that she was okay, getting used to life alone in that big house.

"You're looking extraordinarily well," he continued, and then complimented her stoic approach.

I wasn't sure Chanel and stoicism had anything to do with one another. But, hey, what did it matter? It was like I wasn't there. I knew where the bouquets went, of course, so I took care of placing them, then took a tiny moment to admire how beautiful they were.

I went to find Rebecca Miller, the new warden, to let her know we'd done the flowers. That was one thing she could cross off her list for tomorrow. She gave me a warm hello and a grateful thanks. I liked Rebecca immensely and immediately felt bad that we'd added her to the list of suspects last night. We spoke often on the phone, making arrangements for wedding and funeral flowers to be delivered, but rarely did we speak face to face.

"I'll come and have a look. It always raises my spirits to see fresh flowers in the church." She was six feet tall, liked to wear floral dresses and flat shoes. "Well, Peony, you've outdone yourself. I really love your casual style. I can spot a Bewitching Blooms creation from miles away."

I laughed. "How nice to have a fan. Keep that up and I'll be agreeing to a lifetime's delivery."

"If only," Rebecca mused. Having got precisely nowhere with Gillian this morning, maybe Rebecca could shed some light on Dolores and the WI and hopefully eliminate herself from the lineup in the process.

As casually as I could muster, I asked how the choir and the rest of the church staff were coping after Dolores's death.

Rebecca said that reactions had been mixed.

"She was quite the divisive figure," I said. "I know she pestered Bernard Drake so terribly he gave up his role as warden." The vicar was still chatting away to Gillian, so I kept my voice low. "Did you experience similar harassment?"

"Not to speak ill of the dead, but she did like to give advice on how we could do better. I believe she genuinely meant well. However, the vicar had a word with Dolores when I agreed to take on the role of churchwarden. Dolores had a lot of respect for the vicar. She offered advice when she could, but she never acted with me the way she had with Bernard."

"But she tried to blame you for the communion wine which was spilled on Elizabeth's altar cloth," I said, recalling the words of Dolores's sorry/not sorry card.

Rebecca's eyes widened in surprise. Had she really not known that's what Dolores was saying? Or was she surprised that I knew? "Me?"

"She said you'd left the wine in the chalice. Forgot to put it away after communion."

"I like to think Dolores is sorry for any trouble she may have caused in her time," she said piously. And then, as though she couldn't help herself, she added, "And of course I didn't leave the wine in the communion goblet. I put it away properly, as I always do."

I turned back to where Gillian and the vicar were still

talking. To my surprise, William had his arm around Gillian's shoulders.

Rebecca followed my gaze.

"He certainly seems very popular with the women in the parish," I said.

But Rebecca just chuckled. "I know that move well. He'll be wanting Gillian to donate to the church."

"You mean put extra in the donation plate at Sunday's service?" I admit I didn't know a lot about how the Anglican church operated.

"Oh, no, no, no." Rebecca leaned in. "Part of the vicar's job is fundraising. We are given a budget and fundraising targets. Gillian Fairfax is very wealthy and, since being recently widowed, has shown more interest in attending church. A large donation from her would go a long way to meeting our annual target. As you can imagine, raffles, charity races, and bake sales don't go as far as one would like them to. Individual donations are the lifeblood of a church like this."

Rebecca gestured to the main hall, and I saw that most of the other women had joined the vicar and Gillian. "They're here to help clean and tidy before tomorrow's service," Rebecca said. "Sunday is our most important day." She hastily added, "Though Tuesday will be a momentous occasion too for Dolores's funeral."

I recognized several of the WI women with whom Gillian was hoping to ingratiate herself, and I watched as the vicar expertly brought the women together. Rebecca was right—the vicar was a smooth talker, and before I knew it (and perhaps Gillian, too), one of the women placed a duster in Gillian's soft right hand and was showing her how to reach the rims of the pillars.

I thought of her overworked maid at Lemmington House and wondered when Gillian Fairfax had last used a duster. If she ever had.

I noticed that Elizabeth Sanderson was part of the group of women. She was dressed all in black and her skin was pale and sallow. She certainly looked the part of mourning best friend, but was it a true image? I thought back to our suspects board—currently she was the prime suspect. How could I find a way of talking to Elizabeth without arousing her suspicions? And then I remembered how upset she was in the graveyard the other day. Could that be the opener? A kindly enquiry of concern? It was worth trying.

As I approached, she was spraying furniture polish and wiping it in distracted circles. I said her name gently, placing a hand on her arm.

She jumped and turned to me. Then she dropped her gaze. "Oh, Peony, I've been meaning to come to your shop, but I hadn't the courage. Whatever must you think of me acting so dreadfully the other day? And ruining your beautiful flowers. I'm so very sorry." Her eyes swam with tears.

"It's okay," I said, no longer searching for a way to talk to her. The poor woman was overflowing with sadness. "You were upset. Anyone would be."

"Yes, but the way I acted. It was dreadful. If only I'd known Dolores wouldn't be with us much longer, I never would have said the things I did. Or acted like that. Whatever must you and your poor mother think of me?"

I assured her we both understood. I said, "Why don't I remake that bouquet for Dolores's funeral? She chose those flowers specially."

Elizabeth's tears overflowed. "Oh, the funeral. Yes. I can't believe she's gone."

I hated to push the weeping woman for information, but the opportunity was right here in front of me. In a low voice, I said, "I saw you at the graveyard the other day and noticed that you were upset."

"I was," she said in an equally low voice, glancing over to where the vicar was still holding court. "I wanted Dolores to be buried near the church, in the spot she had picked out, so I could always keep an eye on her grave and tend to it. But William explained that he has to manage the burial ground, so it wasn't possible. I understand his reasoning, of course, and now that I've time to think it over, I've calmed down. I'm certain Dolores will understand. The vicar always knows best." Then she brightened. "He's asked me to embroider some new vestments for Christmas. I'm so pleased."

Then she said, "I shall pray for the poor young man who killed Dolores. Such a terrible thing."

CHAPTER 22

*D*olores Prescott's funeral took place the following Tuesday. The day was overcast, still warm but with puffs of clouds dotted around a muted sky. It was hard not to imagine that it was Dolores's bad mood hanging over us. Elizabeth Sanderson might be resigned to her friend being buried at the back of the graveyard, surrounded by ragwort, but I doubted Dolores would be too pleased.

It was a quiet service and a somber affair, as you can well imagine. Although Dolores wasn't much liked in the village, the dramatic end to her life had shaken everyone up, and they came together both to mark her life and in solidarity as a community. Her murder had rocked our sleepy village.

I wish that I'd been able to set my mind at rest, that the murderer had been detained by the police. But unlike the rest of the Willowers, I didn't think Mick was our man. Thank goodness for Char, Hilary, and my mom. The four of us sat together at the service, but as the reception in the church hall got underway, we were inevitably pulled in different directions. The WI had done most of the flowers for the service, so

I hadn't been involved in the preparations. It gave me more of a chance to mingle, and I chatted while helping myself to the egg and cress sandwiches.

As with many receptions, the conversation was mostly full of platitudes. People were stretching to find nice things to say about Dolores. She had been a good knitter. A committed WI member. Former churchwarden.

Hilary struck up a conversation with Bernard Drake about classical music. Of course, every time I stepped into a church with my mom, I was worried about her talking to spirits. Luckily, she had cornered Gillian—no doubt to try to squeeze extra information from her about Dolores and their petty exchange about the WI.

I was left to watch the scene and eat yet another sandwich when I caught the pleasant aroma of a familiar scent. I turned and there was Alex. He was wearing a charcoal suit, white shirt, and a dark tie, his hair swept back from his face. He must have caught the sun over the weekend, and I bit back the urge to ask him where he'd been. I hadn't seen Alex since the dawn of Saturday morning. I realized now that I'd been hoping to receive a phone call or a text.

"Hi," he said a little shyly.

"Well, hello there," I replied. I didn't know how to act. Should I give him a hug? A peck on the cheek? A hearty handshake?

But Alex swept through my awkwardness and bent to lightly kiss me on the cheek. I can tell you that a beautiful shiver like water rippled through me.

"It was a good send-off," Alex said of the service.

I agreed and told him that the vicar certainly had a way

with words. He was able to tell an extraordinary story about an ordinary life.

"I wanted to let you know that the contract with Monsieur Gagneux was signed. I was going to send you flowers as a thank you, except that would be entirely the wrong gift under the circumstances."

I laughed, although I got that one all the time.

Alex cleared his throat, and I noticed he was a bit less assured than usual. "So in lieu of flowers, I was wondering if I could take you for dinner, properly, as a thank you."

I was surprised by the offer but in the best way possible. "Of course," I said. "That would be lovely." Okay, it still wasn't really a date, but I was getting closer to Alex and it felt good. More than good. It felt right.

I noticed then that something had shifted in the atmosphere of the room. Alex had noticed, too. We both glanced around at the same time and saw that the detectives, Rawlins and Evans, had walked into the reception. A murmur went through the small crowd, and I felt that everyone straightened themselves automatically. What was it about detectives that made even the most innocent feel guilty when they walked into a room?

"I wonder why they're here," Alex said quietly. "Surely, it's not standard practice to attend the funeral as well as lead the investigation?"

I told him that I wasn't sure, but it did seem odd. "Do you think they're realizing that Mick isn't their man?"

Before he could answer, Char came rushing up to us both. Addressing Alex, she asked if he could talk to one of the detectives on Mick's behalf. "He's starting to get desperate. He phones me whenever he can and keeps begging me to help him."

"I'm not sure how I could help," Alex said sadly.

"You're like, a baron, right? Don't people listen to you for that alone? I mean, you're like royalty."

"Char!" I admonished.

But Alex smiled. "It doesn't work that way, I'm afraid."

Poor Char. She was hearing that phrase a lot these days.

The vicar was surrounded by the usual group of women, who seemed to spend a lot of their spare time looking after him. As soon as he saw Alex, he quietly disentangled himself and came toward us, his gaze focused on Alex, of course. Another parishioner who could write a check that would easily solve the year's funding problems.

"Alex. Good to see you," he said in his charming way.

"Wonderful service, Vicar," Alex replied.

And in that moment, everything became clear to me. It's hard to explain, but it was like time slowed down and all the pieces of the puzzle which had been floating around all came together. I took a deep breath.

The vicar turned to me and said, "And your flowers were beautiful, as always."

I hadn't done many, in fact, but it was the sort of kind comment he always made. "Thank you. But, Vicar, we're having a problem," I said. "Perhaps you could help."

"Of course, Peony. How can I be of service?"

Char was standing there appearing puzzled as I explained about Mick and how he wanted his innocence proven.

"But I understand the young man was already wanted for other crimes. Surely he'd be best to pay his penance." He smiled down at Char. "I'll pray for him, of course."

Hmm. As much as I wasn't Mick's biggest fan, I was tired of him being tarred with the same brush as Owen Jones had been. Surely, past mistakes had been atoned for. And paying for the crimes he had committed was not the same as being sentenced for a murder he hadn't.

I raised my voice loud enough that the chatter nearby stopped. "You know all about paying penance, don't you, Vicar?"

He looked taken aback. "In my work, of course."

"You also dish it out, don't you?"

"Gracious me, Peony, whatever has gotten into you? Are you feeling all right?" His expression became genuinely concerned.

I wasn't feeling so good, actually, but I'd started now and everyone was staring at me. I had no place to go but forward. I felt Alex beside me, a silent supportive presence, and that helped. Char might not have a clue what stunt I was pulling, but she was my little sister and had my back. Hilary and Jessie Rae were both looking my way and a flash of blue and yellow from the corner of my eye informed me that Norman had, as usual, ignored my order to stay outside.

"At Bewitching Blooms, I see all the same emotions you do." I glanced around at my friends and neighbors. "I see people when they're happy, thankful, loving, and when they're grieving. I have flowers for all those moods."

"Good ones, too," a man's voice piped up, which I thought was nice of him.

"I also see them when they're sorry for what they've done. When they show humility. It's an important quality, humility. But I'm not so sure you agree."

"Of course, I think humility is important." He glanced

around. "Would you like to make an appointment to see me in private, Peony?" He clearly thought I'd lost the plot. And from the way most of his parishioners were staring at me, they thought so, too.

"But that's not how you run your church, Vicar, is it? With humility. You enjoy the authority too much. You like making the final decisions."

"My calling often involves making final decisions."

"Like burying Dolores in the back of the church among noxious weeds?"

There was an audible gasp, and I realized that the whole room had fallen silent.

The vicar cleared his throat. His cheeks were reddening. "There was no space elsewhere. I've been pruning the patch of ragwort myself."

"I don't think that's true. I think it's because you're punishing Dolores in death, just as you did in life. Dolores *did* destroy Elizabeth's beautiful altar cloth deliberately, and you were so enraged you killed her as punishment."

CHAPTER 23

*I*f I'd wanted to add drama and excitement to the funeral of a murder victim, I'd definitely succeeded.

A ripple of shock rocked the church hall.

The vicar was fully red in the face. "That's absurd. Dolores said it was an accident."

"But you know it wasn't. There was no way the communion wine would have been in the chalice without someone putting it there. Dolores was so jealous that Elizabeth Sanderson would be covered in glory for embroidering that beautiful altar cloth that she deliberately planned to destroy it and make it look like an accident."

"I can't believe she'd do such a wicked thing," Elizabeth wailed.

"But she did. Dolores, as a former warden, knew exactly how to ruin that cloth in a way that appeared accidental. Worse, she didn't just act on an impulse of jealousy but planned the sabotage."

Elizabeth cried even louder, "My beautiful work. Destroyed."

"You were right, Elizabeth. She did ruin that cloth deliberately. She had to sneak into the vestry to get the communion wine and fill the chalice. She knew you were going to the church to measure the cloth before stitching the hem because you told her so. I was right there and so was the vicar. Sometime between then and choir practice, Dolores filled the goblet and set it on the altar. Then, when you were busy measuring, she 'accidentally' knocked it over, spilling the red wine all over your work."

"Why would she do something so terrible?" Rebecca Miller asked.

"Because she really was that jealous. And worse, she tried to blame the accident on you. She claimed you must have left the wine in the goblet. Even in her apology note to Elizabeth, she said it was your fault, not hers."

"Why not accuse Elizabeth of murdering her friend if you're so keen to blame one of us?" the vicar asked.

At that, Elizabeth's wet eyes grew wide with fear. "I didn't do anything. I swear it. I know what I said about revenge, but it was just silly talk. Nonsense."

"I know," I said. "Because you, Elizabeth, truly did learn forgiveness. And you, Vicar, probably helped her with that while you decided to play God. It was Bernard Drake who told me about the three Gs that corrupt a man of the cloth. *Girls, Gold, and God. Women or money have ruined many a good man. And some of them even come to believe they are God, not His servant.*"

"This is insanity," the vicar spat. "You're ruining Dolores's reception with this nonsense."

And then Rebecca Miller spoke up again. Shaking slightly, she said, "I saw you go to Dolores's house the afternoon she was killed. I didn't think anything of it, but I wondered why you never mentioned it when the police were questioning us."

"That's right, sir," Sergeant Evans said, coming up behind him. "You didn't mention to us that you'd seen the victim so close to when she was killed."

"I only went to speak to her about what she'd done. To counsel her. I'm sorry I forgot to mention it. In the drama of the moment, it must have slipped my mind."

Suddenly, I felt like I could see the whole scene. "Maybe you did go to counsel her, but she wasn't playing the part of penitent supplicant, was she? She kept passing the blame on to the new warden. That must have made you furious. Dolores was such a backstabber that you decided to punish her in exactly that way. You stabbed her in the back."

The vicar was shaking his head vehemently. "No, no, no."

"Come, William," Rebecca said. "You must set an example for all of us and do what's right. Tell us. Tell us everything. No matter how it pains you."

"They do say confession is good for the soul, sir," Sergeant Evans said.

"I'm not Catholic," the vicar retorted angrily.

Everyone was staring at him, and for once, he seemed speechless.

"No doubt, once we search your home, we'll find evidence to prove you murdered Dolores Prescott," DI Rawlins said. "Our forensics team is very good."

Suddenly, he wilted. "Oh, very well. I removed a noxious weed from the garden of this divine parish, and I don't regret it. Everything else I have to say, I'll say to the police in private."

The detectives took out their handcuffs and read the vicar his rights as his congregation stood watching in stunned silence.

Norman flew into the hall and landed on Char's shoulder next to me. "Wow. You sure can liven up a funeral, Cookie."

CHAPTER 24

*A*lex opened another bottle of chilled white wine and topped up our glasses. After the drama of Dolores's service, I'd invited everyone to decompress back at the farmhouse—including Alex. To my surprise, he accepted the invitation and now the six of us were sitting outside in the garden, debriefing. The finished stone path was glorious, and with Owen's help, I was turning the garden into a colorful space that attracted butterflies, bees, and friends who needed to debrief after a dramatic day.

Alex had loosened his tie and unbuttoned the top button of his shirt, looking perfectly at home in my garden. And I was finally calming down after I'd accused the vicar of murder in front of the entire village.

Alex must have felt my gaze, for he turned to me and I felt a spurt of happiness. I wondered where he'd take me to dinner, and when. I was sure it would be somewhere fantastic, but not too showy. What the fates had in store for us, I didn't know. There were plenty of issues between us, with him being a werewolf and me being a witch, but right now, I didn't want to think about problems. Only enjoy the day and the company.

"I still don't understand how you knew it was the vicar," Owen said, shaking his head. "It's like you have a sixth sense or something."

Char shot me a look. Jessie Rae was too busy scratching Blue behind the ears to notice anything that anyone non-feline said.

I shook my head. "Not a sixth sense, more like a good memory. It all started to make sense to me after Bernard Drake had explained about the three Gs that corrupt a man of the cloth. Girls, Gold, and God. As soon as he told me that women or money had ruined many a good man, including clergymen corrupted by the power they have over their parish, then certain moments about the vicar's behavior flooded back to me. He was surrounded by women, but he always acted appropriately. He was a good fundraiser, but there was no suggestion of mismanagement. But when I thought about him seeing himself as God, I began to see the pattern."

"But why kill Dolores?" Hilary wanted to know. "Did he go to visit her in order to punish her for her crime?"

I'd wondered the same thing. "I don't think he did mean to kill Dolores, but when she refused to play the penitent role he'd assigned for her, he went a bit crazy, I think."

"I'll say," Norman said. "More cuckoo than the cuckoo."

I continued, "Many of us saw the rage and despair Elizabeth went through, and Elizabeth was one of the vicar's favorites. Also, remember, when Dolores destroyed the altar cloth, she didn't only hurt Elizabeth. The vicar must have seen it as a crime against him and his church. But when he accused her, I'm betting she kept blaming Rebecca Miller. She'd probably taken him into the kitchen to make tea, and no doubt there was a knife handy, and he acted in the heat of the moment. That's my theory, anyway."

Despite my hunch about the vicar, it had still been a shock to watch him being taken away by the police. Reverend William Wadlow had been a stalwart of the community. With wise eyes and a pleasant face, he had conducted himself with decorum, at least in public, ever since we'd first met. He presided over all of the village's keystone events and was available to listen and advise on any issue. The older women in the village loved to fawn over him, and he'd always acted with grace and humility. But that humility had been worn away over the years as he became convinced of his own power.

As he was led away, the women who'd looked after him since his wife died had appeared especially shocked, not least of all poor Elizabeth Sanderson. She'd embroidered a beautiful cloth for the altar, and it had ended in murder. I hoped that the other women in the WI would help her in the coming difficult days. Tomorrow, I would send her flowers with healing properties to help her heart mend.

Char's cell phone began to ring. "That'll be the prison. I'll be right back."

Although I'd spent the last week defending Mick against his accusers, I still didn't like him. The uneasy feeling which had prickled across my skin the moment I'd first laid eyes on Mick hadn't left me. Everything about him had proclaimed *don't mess with me*. And something about his stare made my whole body shiver. But the fear and vulnerability I'd sensed buried deep within him had resulted in an opportunistic young man who was destined to repeat past mistakes until he faced his insecurities and the more fearful side of his nature. If only Mick had invested time working on himself while he was hiding out in Willow Waters, then he might not have attempted to rob Dolores's cottage and got himself mixed up in a murder investigation.

When Char returned, I asked what was going to happen to Mick now.

Char frowned as if mixed up. "Of course, he's delighted that he's no longer a murder suspect. But he's still going to have to face charges relating to the burglaries."

Owen was nodding. "There's only so long you can run for. Everyone has to deal with the consequences of their actions sooner or later."

Hilary agreed.

"True," Char admitted, playing with her silver snake earring, which dangled halfway to her shoulder. "But the police already know he only drove the getaway car. Besides, Hilary came through for us and found him a good lawyer."

"With luck," Hilary said, "he won't have too harsh a sentence. A couple of years, maybe."

I turned to Jessie Rae, who'd been suspiciously quiet while we all put in our two cents but saw that she was utterly transfixed by something behind me. I turned. All I saw was the fridge. What on earth had caught her attention?

And then Blue started hissing. Now my sweet marmalade is a gentle, sleepy creature. She barely mewls, let alone hisses. There was only one thing which never failed to set her off.

"Mom, who do you see?"

But Jessie Rae ignored me. She started swaying back and forth in her chair.

"It seems as if your mother is having one of her visions," Alex said, not unkindly. If anything, Alex tolerated my mom's visions with more empathy than most others in the village, who either rolled their eyes or snickered.

Now I knew why. Not only did Alex have a famous nose, he had all the heightened senses of a werewolf.

"Not a vision, darlin'," Jessie Rae said, rising to her feet and shooing the still-hissing Blue away.

I bent and picked up Blue protectively, and she quietened in my arms.

"But my goodness, Peony," Jessie Rae said, "there's a spirit hovering behind your head." She squinted. "Why, I do believe it's Dolores. And she's...smiling!"

"Cool," Char said. "We exposed her murderer, and now she's thanking us."

"Really?" I asked, surprised at how relieved I was that Dolores had found peace and come to tell us.

"Ooh yes," Jessie Rae confirmed. "And now she's doing a jig and clapping."

"Then," Norman piped up, "she's having more fun in the afterlife than she ever did in this one."

"And let that be a lesson to all of us," Jessie Rae said. "You must enjoy every minute you have in this life."

I glanced up to find Alex's gaze on me. I had a dinner invitation from the most interesting man in the village. I definitely planned to enjoy every minute.

Thanks for reading *Karma Camellia*. I hope you'll consider leaving a review, it really helps. Keep reading for a sneak peek of the next mystery, *Highway to Hellebore,* Village Flower Shop Book 3.

~

Highway to Hellebore, Chapter 1

THINGS DON'T MOVE QUICKLY in a village like Willow Waters, in the Cotswolds, one of England's prettiest areas. To give you just one example out of countless options, when we voted to change the hanging baskets on the high street from the traditional geraniums and blue lobelia to plants more local to the UK, the discussions of what to replace them with were so long and heated that we missed an entire summer.

Yup, that's right. Not a single hanging basket graced our much-photographed and heavily praised high street.

Our indecision (and lack of urgency) dented our pride at being the most gorgeous village in the vicinity and I, for one, made sure not to let the slow pace around here get the better of me again.

But one thing was guaranteed to shatter our peace. A speeding car. So, when a fancy sports model roared by one June morning at top speed, it was a shock.

I had driven myself and Charity Abbot—who goes by Char, *thank-you-very-much*—and her parrot familiar, Norman, to the high street of Willow Waters where my flower shop is located. Char worked at Café Roberto, just down the road from Bewitching Blooms, which is my pride and joy. Well, that's not completely true. Really, my farmhouse is my pride and joy, or it will be when I get it completely renovated.

But the shop is where I create and sell gorgeous bouquets

of flowers—adding a little witchy magic to the blooms to help the recipients, whether they be celebrating a birthday or mourning someone who's passed. We witches are never allowed to use our magic for personal gain. That's a real no-no, but I believe that adding some extra care—for people who need it—falls into the benevolence category.

I know what you're thinking, but the success of Bewitching Blooms isn't due to magic. Believe me, running a successful business in these times takes more than even my best goodwill spells. We do a great job because we work hard and we care about what we do.

The 'we' here includes my brilliantly (and classically) trained florist, Imogen Billings, who I value as my assistant. My business MBA means I'm better at the general running of the shop and throwing together those bouquets that literally look like they were just thrown together. Still, that casual look does take some talent and time to get right.

Anyway, back to the morning in question. Char and I got out of my beaten-up Range Rover, which also doubles as my delivery van, when the low hum of an intensely powerful sports-car engine could be heard. In less time than it took me to register the rumbling sound, a bright-red flash sped past, practically breaking the sound barrier.

As I said, "Wow, that's a—" Char piped up with, "Lamborghini Aventador Coupe. A real beauty."

I'd been going to say sports car.

Char was extremely conversant with cars. She could identify the year and model from far away. And fix them, too, if need be. She'd been working on the old Citroën truck my husband, Jeremy, had bought just before he died. It had pretty much been a garden ornament, or garden shed ornament really, until she took it apart piece by piece and put it together again. Now it ran perfectly well, and we considered it her vehicle. Char, who was barely in her twenties, named it Frodo.

Parking spots in the village were highly prized, so it was easier for Char to ride in with me and then walk the remaining distance to her job as a barista.

We were both still staring into the distance where the Lamborghini had swiftly disappeared when she said, "I know there's a lot of rich people around here, but a model like that would likely set you back a cool two hundred and eighty grand."

I sucked in my breath. Nearly three hundred thousand pounds? For a car?

There were a lot of wealthy people who had first or second homes in our pretty little village in the Cotswolds. Plenty of them commuted a couple of times a week into London for their fancy jobs in finance, media, or tech—but the Italian Riviera, this was not. With the odd exception, people tended to play down their wealth here, as any show of ostentation was frowned upon in a very British way.

So, this vehicle was certainly new in town. My instinct was to hope that it would keep going. And at the rate they were driving, they'd be in Edinburgh by lunchtime.

Order your copy today! *Highway to Hellebore* is Book 3 in the Village Flower Shop series.

A Note from Nancy

Dear Reader,

Thank you for reading *Karma Camellia*. I hope you'll consider leaving a review and please tell your friends who like flowers and paranormal cozy mysteries. Review on Amazon, Goodreads or BookBub.

If you enjoy knitting and paranormal cozy mysteries, you might also enjoy *The Vampire Knitting Club* - a story that NYT Bestselling Author Jenn McKinlay calls "a delightful paranormal cozy mystery perfectly set in a knitting shop in Oxford, England. With intrepid, late blooming amateur sleuth, Lucy Swift, and a cast of truly unforgettable characters, this mystery delivers all the goods."

Join my newsletter for a free prequel, *Tangles and Treasons*, the exciting tale of how the gorgeous Rafe Crosyer, from *The Vampire Knitting Club* series, was turned into a vampire.

I hope to see you in my private Facebook Group. It's a lot of fun. www.facebook.com/groups/NancyWarrenKnitwits

Until next time,
Happy Reading,

Nancy

ALSO BY NANCY WARREN

The best way to keep up with new releases, plus enjoy bonus content and prizes is to join Nancy's newsletter at NancyWarrenAuthor.com or join her in her private Facebook group Nancy Warren's Knitwits.

Village Flower Shop: Paranormal Cozy Mystery

In a picture-perfect Cotswold village, flowers, witches, and murder make quite the bouquet for flower shop owner Peony Bellefleur.

Peony Dreadful - Book 1

Karma Camellia - Book 2

Highway to Hellebore - Book 3

Luck of the Iris - Book 4

Vampire Knitting Club: Paranormal Cozy Mystery

Lucy Swift inherits an Oxford knitting shop and the late-night knitting club vampires who live downstairs.

Tangles and Treasons - a free prequel for Nancy's newsletter subscribers

The Vampire Knitting Club - Book 1

Stitches and Witches - Book 2

Crochet and Cauldrons - Book 3

Vampire Knitting Club: Cornwall: Paranormal Cozy Mystery

Boston-bred witch Jennifer Cunningham agrees to run a knitting and yarn shop in a fishing village in Cornwall, England—with characters from the Oxford-set *Vampire Knitting Club* series.

Vampire Book Club: Paranormal Women's Fiction Cozy Mystery

Seattle witch Quinn Callahan's midlife crisis is interrupted when she gets sent to Ballydehag, Ireland, to run an unusual bookshop.

Crossing the Lines - Prequel

The Vampire Book Club - Book 1

Chapter and Curse - Book 2

A Spelling Mistake - Book 3

A Poisonous Review - Book 4

Great Witches Baking Show: Paranormal Culinary Cozy Mystery

Poppy Wilkinson, an American with English roots, joins a reality show to win the crown of Britain's Best Baker—and to get inside Broomewode Hall to uncover the secrets of her past.

The Great Witches Baking Show - Book 1

Baker's Coven - Book 2

A Rolling Scone - Book 3

A Bundt Instrument - Book 4

Blood, Sweat and Tiers - Book 5

Crumbs and Misdemeanors - Book 6

A Cream of Passion - Book 7

Cakes and Pains - Book 8

Whisk and Reward - Book 9

Gingerdead House - A Holiday Whodunnit

The Great Witches Baking Show Boxed Set: Books 1-3

The Great Witches Baking Show Boxed Set: Books 4-6 (includes bonus novella)

The Great Witches Baking Show Boxed Set: Books 7-9

Toni Diamond Mysteries

Toni Diamond is a successful saleswoman for Lady Bianca Cosmetics in this series of humorous cozy mysteries.

Frosted Shadow - Book 1

Ultimate Concealer - Book 2

Midnight Shimmer - Book 3

A Diamond Choker For Christmas - A Holiday Whodunnit

Toni Diamond Mysteries Boxed Set: Books 1-4

The Almost Wives Club: Contemporary Romantic Comedy

An enchanted wedding dress is a matchmaker in this series of romantic comedies where five runaway brides find out who the best men really are.

The Almost Wives Club: Kate - Book 1

Secondhand Bride - Book 2

Bridesmaid for Hire - Book 3

The Wedding Flight - Book 4

If the Dress Fits - Book 5

The Almost Wives Club Boxed Set: Books 1-5

Take a Chance: Contemporary Romance

Meet the Chance family, a cobbled together family of eleven kids who are all grown up and finding their ways in life and love.

Chance Encounter - Prequel

Kiss a Girl in the Rain - Book 1

Iris in Bloom - Book 2

Blueprint for a Kiss - Book 3

Every Rose - Book 4

Love to Go - Book 5

The Sheriff's Sweet Surrender - Book 6

The Daisy Game - Book 7

Take a Chance Boxed Set: Prequel and Books 1-3

Abigail Dixon Mysteries: 1920s Cozy Historical Mystery

In 1920s Paris everything is très chic, except murder.

Death of a Flapper - Book 1

For a complete list of books, check out Nancy's website at
NancyWarrenAuthor.com

ABOUT THE AUTHOR

Nancy Warren is the USA Today Bestselling author of more than 100 novels. She's originally from Vancouver, Canada, though she tends to wander and has lived in England, Italy, and California at various times. While living in Oxford she dreamed up *The Vampire Knitting Club*. Favorite moments include being the answer to a crossword puzzle clue in Canada's National Post newspaper, being featured on the front page of the New York Times when her book Speed Dating launched Harlequin's NASCAR series, and being nominated three times for Romance Writers of America's RITA award. She has an MA in Creative Writing from Bath Spa University. She's an avid hiker, loves chocolate, and most of all, loves to hear from readers!

The best way to stay in touch is to sign up for Nancy's newsletter at NancyWarrenAuthor.com or www.facebook.com/groups/NancyWarrenKnitwits

To learn more about Nancy and her books
NancyWarrenAuthor.com

facebook.com/AuthorNancyWarren

twitter.com/nancywarren1

instagram.com/nancywarrenauthor

amazon.com/Nancy-Warren/e/B001H6NM5Q

goodreads.com/nancywarren

bookbub.com/authors/nancy-warren

Printed in Great Britain
by Amazon

51892961R10123